11:9 are publishing *Glasgow Kiss* with support from Glasgow City Council. The first book of its kind to come from Glasgow, this celebratory volume of short stories was selected from work submitted by Glasgow's many writing groups.

11:9 is dedicated to launching new writers into the market-place and we are delighted to present 20 new writers in this anthology.

Glasgow Kiss

a collection of new writing from Glasgow

First published by

303a The Pentagon Centre
36 Washington Street
GLASGOW
G3 8AZ

Tel: 0141 204 1109
Fax: 0141 221 5363

E-mail: info@nwp.sol.co.uk
www.11-9.co.uk

A catalogue record for this book is available from the British Library

11:9 is funded by the Scottish Arts Council National Lottery Fund

The publishers are grateful for the support of Glasgow City Council and Glasgow's writers' groups

ISBN 1 903238-33-1

Typeset in Utopia
Printed in Glasgow by Omnia Books

Contents

Foreword

by Edwin Morgan
poet laureate for Glasgow

Glasgow is well provided with writers' groups, and this collection of stories by group members gives excellent proof of the vigour of their activities. No such communal help was on offer when I began writing, many years ago, and although there will always be some who prefer to work away by themselves, 'for like a mole I journey in the dark' like John Davidson's clerk, making their mistakes and gradually getting better, there is no doubt that much talent can be drawn out and nurtured through friendly group exposure and encouraging criticism. The groups represented here come from many different parts of the city, some attached to institutions like libraries and universities, some not. Overall, they have delivered a remarkably varied and confident batch of tales which the public can be invited to enjoy.

Settings range from Glasgow and Berlin to Applecross and the Solway Firth, though the emphasis, as one might expect, is on things Glaswegian, from the humdrum to the bizarre. Some people are looking for Job Centres, others are looking for fetish clubs. That's life, Jim, as we know it. It is good to see this willingness to step outside the uncharmed circle of stereotyped places and images. There is plenty of real observation in these stories, and real probing of recognisable characters, but there is also a nice leavening of imagination, and imagination is of great importance, sometimes neglected as it is by those who want to insist on the truth of 'experience'.

If you want to write about a talking dog which claims to be a Native American Great Spirit, you must feel free to do so (*Pipe Dreams*). If you want to disappear in a truly fey Highland way by creeping into a hinged coffin sliding overboard from a trawler, go ahead, give the local police problems (*A Drop in the Ocean*)! If you can evoke something of the very ancient strangeness of Hallowe'en by taking your readers to meet a skeletal black-cowled ferryman on the Yoker Ferry, set out and be not a-fear'd (*The Ferrymaster*).

Such stories are well balanced by the more ordinary themes: sitting on a park bench, taking children to the Barras, making porridge, going to a party, listening to a gossipy hairdresser, playing bingo, having a crush on a teacher. There are some sharp eyes and ears among the writers of these tales.

A tradition of Glasgow violence is not much in evidence but does make an almost statutory appearance in *Wee Sparra Gets His Wings Clipped,* a well-told vengeance piece with a sectarian background and a twist in the ending. The fact that this story is not without some touches of humour is perhaps a pointer to the flavour of the collection as a whole, where humour, either gallus or sly, is seldom far off. Readers can be warmly welcomed to this anthology, and the writers themselves, seeing their work in print, should find the experience both rewarding and encouraging.

Edwin Morgan
August 2001

Glasgow Kiss

Doors

Sheila Puri

The bag was stuck. It just wouldn't budge. The queue behind him was impatient to get off. Fifteen minutes earlier he'd just managed to jump on the train before the porter slammed the last door shut, and he had hurriedly shoved the bag wherever he could. Then it had slipped easily between two seats. The fat man next to him sniffed. Just, just for this moment, Mr Singh was too happy at catching the train and too exhausted to let the old man's distaste bother him.

People behind him shuffled their feet, muttered under their breath and in other quiet ways made their annoyance felt. Back in India they would have acted differently, pushed, shouted at him to hurry up, even swore. Somebody who liked to be in the centre of things – and lots in India did – would have come and helped. Meanwhile he could have glared at the hostile ones. He then would have felt human and honest. But here people behaved differently. They smiled and said nice day but made damn sure that you didn't get near them. Especially living next door. Foreigners are always unwelcome.

Remembering this added enough extra discomfort to make Mr Singh's head really hot beneath his maroon turban. It caused a film of wetness at the back of his neck. He turned to look behind and saw a line of white faces watching him, an Indian with dark skin and a bright turban. Immediately he gave the bag a hard yank and the bulked-up plastic sprang towards him and hit his knee hard. The pain shot up to his head. He ignored it as much as he could and straightened up, gripped the handle of his bag and walked towards the door. The others followed quietly behind, seeming satisfied.

Outside the station he saw block upon block of grey concrete, dark windows and closed wooden doors. In Moga doors and shutters were left open letting any passer-by look in at people sitting in courtyards peeling and chopping vegetables for the evening meal, folding clothes that had been left out to dry on the flat roofs underneath a scorching sun. Here, he didn't know what was behind the concrete walls. Being a door-to-door salesman wasn't easy.

He crossed some empty streets, not noticing the skeleton trees spaced evenly along the edges of the pavements. He stopped in a street called Redgment Street and went to the first house: the gate had a number one painted on to it in fancy lettering.

Already the place felt alien to him. His arms tensed as soon as the gravel path sounded under his feet. Reaching the door, he noticed the sweet sickliness of Lux Flakes and the smell left a day after cakes had been baked. Mrs O'Brien, who rented a room next to him and his cousin, was always baking, and she used to give them roly-polies, spotted dicks and apple pies, warm out of the oven. This smell only reminded him of how much of an outsider he was, and it too became a threat. Standing at that front door, Mr Singh's neck became poker hot and his feet icy cold.

He pressed the bell and waited, heart beating in his ears. No answer, stillness. He pressed again, the only sound the trrring of the bell. He tried one more time, but still no answer. The build-up had been futile and he felt stupid and let down, almost embarrassed as if someone had seen him and knew the way he was feeling. Eventually his heart began to slow down, the heat from his body subsided and the muscles in his arms, back and legs loosened again. His head fell slightly forward.

He rang a few more bells. A few doors were answered with 'My mum isn't in', said in grating, sneering voices. By the eleventh house, the bag began to feel very heavy. A boy of ten stood behind the lace curtain aping a monkey and shouting at him while the shadow of an adult stood further back with folded arms. Mr Singh's head and arms felt engulfed in flames. If anyone had looked at his face, they would have seen shame and self-loathing in his eves. A hardness formed in his chest and he tried not to think – to think would have meant feeling. Physical pain he could bear, any other kind he could not. He walked out of the garden aware of the gaze of the boy and woman searing into his back. He almost hid in the porch of the next house.

As he stood in front of this new door trying to get rid of or at least hide the feelings which the last house had left, he desperately wanted to run and hide, to leave all this behind. But he had no choice but to carry on ringing bells and facing the outcome. His sweaty hand pressed the bell. A woman answered. He was so glad that someone had opened their door that he immediately started his set speech:

'I have toys, clothes, jam...'

The woman looked bored and ready to shut the door, so he quickly added, 'All very cheap, cheap baby shoes, only a shilling a pair...'

She paused, and the look in her eyes told him she was interested. Mr Singh's insides jumped and he became alive with hope.

'Let's have a look then,' she said.

He knelt down by his bag and unzipped it, pushing shirts, bottles of jam, packets of stockings aside, searching for the baby shoes. Then he saw them snuggled between a packet of Peek Freans and a tin of razor blades. He was glad that he carried a lot of different things with him, especially when he got a sale. He brought out the clear plastic box and handed it to the woman, hoping that she would like them.

She stood looking at them, turning the box slowly around. When asked, Mr Singh was only too glad to take the shoes out for her. He watched her touching the satin fabric and waited, waited, his insides tensing, just hoping, and at last she said, 'Yes, I'll take them. A shilling, you said? I must say, you people are cheap. I think I'll take two, girls round here are always having weans. You'd think they had nothing else to do.'

She continued talking in this way while Mr Singh got another pair of shoes out and handed them to her. By now she had moved on to remarking on how hard working his people were. 'If our boys worked half as hard.'

At the first opportunity, Mr Singh said apologetically, 'Two shillings, please,' and she stopped and went inside for her purse.

He repacked the bag. Everything slipped easily into place and he was ready to try the next house with enthusiasm. But reality returned with each step towards the gate. So far he'd only had one sale and he needed many more before he could even repay the airfare loan.

The day grew darker, its dull greyness broken only by the yellow-orange streetlights above him. He managed to sell a few pairs of stockings, a jar of marmalade and some razors. A few people asked for things he didn't have and he said he'd bring them next time. He was determined to succeed. Eventually, his head drooping with weariness, he trudged back to the station.

The clock's round whiteness, hanging from chains above the platform, showed the time; one hand pointed to viii and the other to v. He didn't recognise the numbers but he could tell it was twenty minutes to six. In five minutes the train was due, so he glanced at the other dark shapes standing on the platform, aloof, safely distanced from one another, silent. He could not have imagined that such stillness was possible with so many people. This country had taught him a lot of new things.

Inside the train the windows were opaque with condensation. Mr Singh sat in an empty seat a couple of rows from the door and placed the large bag on his knee. He wiped the moisture from the window and saw, staring sideways at him, a thin face with a maroon turban. His head almost jerked back at the sight of a strange face, so unlike those he had seen all day. It took him a few seconds to realise he was looking at his own reflection.

He turned quickly away from the window to face the green plastic of the seat in front of him. The seats began to fill. People glanced at the space next to him and walked past. At last only two seats were left, the one by him and another, five rows ahead. A large woman with a baby walked past him to the seat further away.

Sitting under the dim lights with the darkness outside, Mr Singh tried again not to think. Instead he put his hand into his pocket and felt the smooth roundness of the coins which he had earned that day. He tried to relax in the corner, but was aware of a tightness in his belly and throat. He could not escape his feelings. To block them out, he closed his eyes, leaned back in his seat and let himself see fields of yellow mustard and feel the hot midday sun. The train rattled on through the dark countryside.

He had the key ready in his hand as he approached the house where he lodged. He shared a room with his cousin who would now be out at work washing dishes in the new Indian restaurant around the corner. There were four rooms altogether. An Irish family with three children had the room next to the kitchen and the other rooms lay empty and locked. The house smelled of a wet washcloth left in a closed cupboard for days. The floor of his room was covered with crumpled blankets and quilts. And patches of plaster showed where the pink wallpaper had peeled away from the walls. A few stained cups lay beside the skirting board.

Mr Singh walked to the far end of the room and, not really knowing why, looked out of the window at the lights and empty street. He immediately turned back and sank to the floor beneath the window. Pulling his knees up to his chin and letting his head fall forward, he huddled there without moving for at least half an hour.

Then he noticed the pain in his groin and realised he needed a pishav.

The toilet was covered with a thin layer of dust and grime and it stank. As he was about to wash his hands, he caught a glimpse of himself in the mirror. No wonder people didn't open their doors to him or buy from him. His thin, dark face, crowned with a massive turban, looked so odd. He didn't fit in.

He began to feel more and more disgusted with himself. Full of anger, he lifted the turban from his head and let it fall, six yards of crumpled muslin, into a heap on the floor. The moment of revulsion passed and he could have stopped himself. But today he felt he had to act before he had time to change his mind. He took the rusting pair of scissors from the cabinet by the sink, lifted them to the coil of hair on the top of his head and cut swiftly.

The hair dropped into his hands and the feel of the mass of slippery strands made him shudder. He wanted to weep. Instead he concentrated on the scissors and his fingers, working them through the blackness, bringing out chunks of hair and throwing them into the sink. Eventually the sink was full, so he combed the remaining hair on his head back from his face.

He looked at himself, the stranger with the short hair and the long beard. He began to hack away at his beard, each time getting closer and closer to his chin, almost pulling the hairs out. He continued in this way for about five minutes and then went back to the hair on his head, taking the scissors to just above and behind the ears, to the top of his neck and as close to his skull as possible. Now he could not see himself in the mirror. And then he looked at the part of himself that lay in the sink and on the floor.

He tidied everything up, gathered the hair and wrapped it in a newspaper ready for the bin. The turban he picked up and folded neatly back in his suitcase. Everything done, he went back to his room and covered himself with the thick quilt his mother had made for him. He remembered his mother and a neighbour travelling to the small market town and haggling for the finest cotton at the best price. They had then spent days compacting, sewing and covering it. The quilt felt warm and safe.

Suddenly his knee started to hurt. He pulled back the quilts, rolled back his trouser leg and saw a purple bruise. When he touched it, he felt a sharp, stabbing pain. His thoughts and feelings broke out, welled up, and he let out what sounded like a stifled cough followed by choking. This grew louder and louder. He began to shake more and more violently, the water from his eyes soaked his face. The moment of defeat had arrived and he pulled the quilt over his head and howled into it, stopping only when he was completely and utterly empty. Mr Singh, the economic refugee, eventually slept.

Tuning In

Ingrid Lees

On our way back home from school we frequently dawdled, my brother and I. There was so much to see, so much time to think and talk. Ruined blocks of flats lined our streets interspersed with houses that were only damaged or even completely intact. That is where all the people lived, crowded together.

But it was the ruins that fascinated us. There we could see the strangest things. High up on a top floor was a bathtub sticking into space, maybe with rain water trickling or splashing through its rusty plug hole, depending on the weather. Loose wallpaper flapped merrily in the wind. Out of reach a chest of drawers was balanced precariously on too narrow a ledge. What could be in the chest? Perhaps a strong wind would send it crashing down and we could discover treasure before everything was taken. A ripped dirty white curtain had been flapping for some years through a window without glass – a tired flag of surrender. And all was so open: no roofs, no walls, no floors, no secrets.

All the time we noticed the ruins changing: more wood salvaged by the brave for warmth, a floor collapsed, another wall crashed down. Grass and weeds, even small trees and bushes had started growing where once people had lived. And fearless rats scuttled about freely. Now these mere skeletons of houses were theirs. Warned about the danger of the ruins collapsing, we only dared to look on from a safe distance as we spun our tales about who had lived there.

As we knew nobody would be at home after school,

another good way to pass the time was to gawp down holes in pavement, dug by workmen. Men were in short supply in our lives. There were hardly any about – some very old ones, yes, but younger men we rarely saw. So we were fascinated by these workmen in dirty overalls down their dank holes. We stood and watched them with curiosity as they worked with their shovels, crowbars and other mysterious tools and speculated on what was happening in their underworld. In the summer heat they would strip off and we admired their strong muscles moving under their brown skin and the sweat running down their bent backs. If we stood downwind their acrid smell would drift into our noses and make us giggle.

They were economical with words, these workmen, and sounded rough as they yelled at one another. When they shouted up to us and waved a shovel like a fly swat, we ran in fear. They very often used words we had never heard before. Soon we knew those words well, but still were not sure of their exact meaning. We had a vague idea we must not use these words ourselves – they were not what Ma and Gran would approve of. It was only later that we tried out those words, one by one, cautiously.

The workmen sometimes erected small tent-like structures beside the holes. We loved peering in through a gap and saw them eating thick pieces of bread from their black hands and slurping water from bottles, or something hot from chipped mugs.

My brother badly wanted to be one of those men when he was grown up, to work all day outside in such a hole and not to have to wash his hands. I was not so sure about that. Anyway, I was a girl and we never saw women down those holes. Also I was a year older. More sensible. That is why I had the key for our flat on a piece of string securely tied around my neck.

This day was no different. On our way back from school we had spent a long time checking the ruins and watching workmen. I was fed up and wanted to go home to do something different. But my brother was glued to a hole.

'Come on now, I'm going home,' I said.

'I'm not,' he answered.

'Well, I've got the key. You can't get in later. I have to get bread.'

'You're just saying it, you mean thing,' he replied and stuck his tongue out at me.

I didn't take any notice and went on my way. I knew the power of that key around my neck. By the time I reached our block of flats my brother was right behind me. We went into our staircase and sucked in the familiar aroma of dust and stale cabbage soup. In our scuffed boots we clattered together up the stairs shouting to each other. Past the ground floor, then up to the sickly offal smells of the first floor where the communist Klopps lived on the right. Old Klopp worked at the abbatoir and brought home all sorts of delicacies in his lunch can that Old Ma Klopp stewed into nourishing soups, making us all feel, at the same time, sick and yet hungry for meaty things. We knew for certain she was at it right now.

When we reached our door on the second floor, directly above the Klopps, I bent down and stuck my magic key, still tied by its string around my neck, into the lock. Before I could turn the key the lock pulled away, jerking my neck, as the door was opened by someone inside the flat. I was scared. Goose pimples and cold sweat crept over me. Thank goodness my brother was there with me. When I looked up, ready to scream, it was my Gran in her old black dress and faded apron. She stood in the doorway with hands on her hips, strong and upright, in full control as always, like the captain of a ship ready to sail. What a relief. I threw my arms around her, hugged her round the middle and buried my face in her bosom. With her knobbly arthritic hands she patted us briefly on our heads.

'Where have you two been all this time? All the other children have been back a long time,' she scalded, stern-faced.

'Oh Gran. We were playing.'

'I know. Roaming the streets. I don't know what has become of you.'

She was strict, our grandmother. No nonsense with her.

'And keep away from those ruins. The bombs have killed lots of people, but the ruins still kill now. And don't talk to the workmen... So many crazy people. That's what the war has done...'

She went on and on as usual. It ran off our backs like rainwater.

'Anyway, just come in and be quiet. It's time for the news already.'

We all went inside and she shut the door. My brother and I did not dare to look at one another. Our bodies started to quiver with giggles as we knew what was to come.

Our Gran read the newspaper and listened to the news on the radio several times every day. She just had to. And we had to be quiet. It seemed funny to us that the news was so important to her, more important than us children. When we made a noise or laughed she became angry. When we asked her why she liked the news so much she would say: 'I've got to know what's going on in the world.'

So Gran went straight to the small brown wooden radio with the cloth front, switched it on and waited while it warmed up. Then she fiddled with the knobs as usual. She was trying to tune to the West Berlin radio station, very quietly, so the neighbours would not hear. In East Berlin listening to a Western radio station was a serious crime. It could have got us all locked up. We were all well used to this system of constant tuning and quiet listening.

This process needed all of Gran's concentration. When she had the right programme, ever so softly, she bent forward so her head was all but in the radio. Her attention was on what came out of the radio. To her, we had all but vanished. Of course, we two looked at each other and could not help sniggering softly. We nudged each other, shoving each other about the room.

'Quiet – the news,' she grunted, angrily.

So we went off to the kitchen, my brother and I, to see if she had brought us something from West Berlin where she lived, where the shops were bright, and full of all sorts. Yes! Wow! White bread! And a whole jar of syrup. I licked my finger in anticipation. We raced back to her. How could we wait any longer for bread and syrup? And we could not just greedily help ourselves, could we?

'Gran?' I whispered.

'Shhh.'

'But Gran.'

'Shh. The news.'

'We're hungry,' piped my brother.

'Just wait, nearly finished.'

'Can't wait. We're starving,' I whispered.

'Shh. It's serious.'

We did not dare to interrupt any more, we looked at her horror-stricken face and waited, frozen, with open mouths.

At the end of the news she switched off and said, 'My God. A bloody war again. Third time for me. And bombed out twice.'

Did I hear right? One of the workmen's words coming out of Gran's mouth. Did she know such words? It did not seem the right time to ask her what the meaning was.

'War? Where?' was all I dared to ask.

'In Korea. It's far away, but wars spread.'

We all three stood quietly, and then Gran said, 'Come on. Let's go and have that bread and syrup while we still can.'

'Gran, don't forget to turn the tuning dial,' we reminded her.

One Recruit Short

E K Reeder

When I run I am lawless. I am an insomniac nightrunner and am outside the laws of what night should contain. When I return in the dawn with the change of night upon me I rouse the suspicions of my neighbours. The running does not really frighten them, but it gives them a good excuse to pass over me the way that they do, eyeing me like it is the foreign city in me that makes me unacceptable.

I do not despair what my new neighbours think because, outside the sleep that has been taken from me, I have become a small town sleepwalker, nightrunner. In the deep country dark the roads are too risky and the fields too uneven, so I choose to climb over Saracen High School's fence and use the outdoor track. This allows me to find the true solidness of running. In the beginning, in the summer, the heat overwhelmed me. As cool autumn arrived, the dark became what I could feel effortless against the skin of my arms.

When I do stumble upon sleep I dream of a woman named Anna. Her smell pulls close around me and the unbelievable smoothness of her skin holds me so strongly that every dark, too early morning when I am woken from this glimpse of sleep, I am amazed that she has not left behind a lost hair or the faint scent of her coconut shampoo on my hands. I check the pillows, pull my hands up to my face, inhale.

In this life I have the running and her presence upon me in the early morning. And a one-bedroom apartment between fields of corn and the rural high school where I teach physics to bored but obnoxious seniors. Kids spot difference instantly, and even if my accent might have been cool, the general air of man-less-ness I unwittingly give off is not. They have heard their parents talking.

In my old life, the one I left behind for no reason other than the need for change, I had a two-bedroom flat in Glasgow's West End. I made my decision to leave before everything we started became inevitable. Anna was a straight, long time friend and we spent my last week in Scotland enthralled between the floor of the living room and my double bed. We were friends and then, somewhere between her acknowledgement of specific desire and my flight to a new life, we were something else. No one was more surprised than me when I was woken up on my first mid-august, heat-stroked, Midwest morning overwhelmed by the memory of a woman who was just testing the waters.

My neighbours here have cars stickered with God brightness and damnation: *The Killing of an Unborn Child is a Sin;* a simple Christian fish; *Jesus Saves;* a cartooned white-hooded cross; and *My Son is an A Student at Saracen High* (you never seem to see those stickers for daughters).

They have loud tiny kids who they largely ignore and let play with the broken pavement in front of the eight-block low apartments. On Friday nights their teenagers drive big-wheeled trucks around the town square, honking song horns and trying to impress.

They are like all neighbours. I hear them fight and laugh and try to talk over their child screaming for attention, again. Nearly all are married and look down on the couples who don't have kids or who are unmarried and living in sin. It's a small town, Christian thing.

I know that if they were to look closely enough they would see who I am written all over my face and embedded in the way that I walk. I keep myself to myself and they try not to look too closely. Once they understand that it is me running on the track at night, what is said about me is not said to my face: I spend my nights in the company of owls who have been known to steal the souls of children.

I may not say much but I am not one to hide. After the first week of seeing people's beliefs festooned on their bumpers, I want to make my own declaration of faith across the back of my Corolla. I search for a month before I find the perfect bumper sticker: *One Recruit Short of a Rowing Crew.* I like it because it plays with common misconceptions of how one in ten becomes *the* one in ten, and because it'll get honks from the right sorts of people.

Nothing. She has sent me an envelope full of nothing.

I stand breathless by the door, the other post scattered at my feet. All lost souls of years past are gathering together and the living are dressing up to greet them. I am looking for the letter of a woman. My clothes hang and cling in new places yet all my new strength does not stop my hands from shaking. I hold onto a plain white envelope with a post-office-blue *par avion* sticker haphazardly stuck across the upper left corner like a warning. She has managed to spell my name correctly, but got the name of the town wrong and left off the state and zip code altogether. Across the flap, on the back where the return address should have been, she has written in scrawling print, BY PLANE.

With so much of the address wrong or gone missing, she

should have simply cut to the chase and written BY SLOW BOAT instead. The date stamp on the front tells me that she has sent it while the taste of me must still have been at her fingertips.

While I have been waiting for months my body has changed into that of a runner's. Insomnia has clarified my vision but I carry around my longing for her like dark baggage beneath my eyes. Anyone can see that I am pining.

And what for? What is it all for? The paper cut as I tried to keep the envelope intact, the small beads of blood which taste mild as I put my finger to my lips and peer inside the empty envelope. What is it for? The loss of sleep, the running, the detritus of love?

It is for nothing in a place where I had expected something. The love of a woman in a letter. The lost suggestion of something more than sex. I thought that maybe she would leave him for me, that maybe I had changed the way she looked at the world. I thought that maybe the earth had moved and she had understood something that had been missing before. I take my finger and run it along the inside of the envelope to look for a small scrap of significance. Nothing: she has sent me what I had been able to give her, absolutely nothing.

I gather all the post together, place it in a drawer and then I get into my costume. I have two big bowls of sweets for my neighbour's children and for my students who will come by to get a glimpse into my living room. I play *All the Things that She Gave Me* at a respectable volume, and put on my false teeth. I don't bother to go to bed at all.

On this particular night that I don't sleep, I don't understand her at all. I run until I am breathless. When I walk to catch my breath, the edges of the dream of her drip down my spine and settle in the fine hairs at the small of my back. I want to be furious at her for the game she is obviously playing. But instead I am a bit curious. It has to mean *something*. If she had sent me a picture, any picture, I would understand. It's worth a thousand words. But nothing? What does nothing mean?

I run on, eyes shut and the smell of heaven upon me, remembering. –I lied to you all those years ago, when you asked me what I would do if I could do something and no one would find out. I lied to you then… I'd already had sex on a train, she grinned. She looked at me sober, not knowing that she had already told me this years ago, with vodka honesty. I interrupted her, –I know, you would want to have sex with a woman just to see how it feels. They've got a label for it now, bi-curious. I didn't say it meanly but just as the fact it was. She was not angry, nor finished. –No Jackie, I want you. She had leaned over, put her hand on my knee. Her kiss was doubtless.

After a week of being something other than we had been before I left on the plane in a clichéd cool-as-a-cucumber fashion. Now I find myself waking up with the presence of a desire I have never known. Head over heels out of bed and onto the night high school track.

It is on that first morning before I start to run that I realise I am in love with her. It is not logical and I try to run myself back to reality.

I have spent months knocking sense into my head through my feet and my legs. I try, with all the strength of my body, to put that week behind me.

For the last class before Thanksgiving weekend I bring in a video and push the tape into the machine. It's fun time. I ask the class to watch carefully and list all the rules of physics, gravity and life that are broken in the sequence that follows. They look at me and think I am mad. When road runner and coyote break into their usual antics they know I am. We watch the sequence five times. It works. Somewhere between the heavy acme package dropping and flattening coyote, and road runner's legs moving like wheels, we all become happier to be where we are.

The rare mornings when I sleep solid and fast are the worst of all. She is not here, I have had no dreams, and no time to find her. I have not had a chance to get to the place that I run to, that place where I no longer have to think about the impossibility of her being here. In the coming light, sweat-drenched after the truth of the dark, I can pretend that she is across the grass, through the thin walls, and lying blissfully asleep in the Wisconsin dawn. But, when I sleep through the dark and I open my eyes to what is so clearly her absence, I am split apart, hard-soled.

Once I don't receive the letter she didn't send, I find small town living a bit easier. I don't worry about the neighbours finding out my secret because, without her, I am simply a rogue single woman. They can make up stories but have no proof. I still carry my baggage beneath my eyes but it no longer looks quite so much like longing, much more like loss.

At Christmas I send her a light letter and I tell her about how I have become sort of attached to my insomnia and night running. The letter is long enough for her to read between the lines. I settle into my life and, after the holidays, the waking continues but the running changes and slows. Winter running is different: slower, more like a layered walk, a brisk snow-giant sort of gait. I take to walking in the fields when the moon is full and the snow gives off enough light to guide me.

On darker nights I stay to the track and run, shedding layers, leaving jackets and track suits by the fence that I climb. I am sifting through what I have been and my footprints mark the finer dust of the future. As I run I know that the first woman you make love with, the first woman you fall in love with, is beautiful and strong and scary and unlike anything you have ever experienced before. She smells of heaven and is more expansive than night. I begin to wonder exactly how you could fit that into an envelope. I run beyond what I am beginning to understand to the peace of space; the home of unknowing and letting go. My lungs are cold with the breathing in of the sky. Bitterly cold winter crisps through leafless branches, the track crackles and the stars are clear with the height of winter's demands.

In February I have a week of truly deep sleep where I dream of other things. I think that I must be getting my life under control. Someone figures out that my bumper sticker means exactly what they thought it might and slashes all four of my tyres. As I am changing them Joe Ford (who has a jesus fish and a Saracen High tiger sticker stretched across his bumper) tells me that I should report the slashings to the police because it doesn't seem right. He means it. He leans lightly on the hood of my car and I can tell that he wants to tell me who did it but is bound by family loyalty. –I hope that they got whatever was bothering them out of their systems because I can't afford another set of tyres, I say. –I'm sure that he has. He looks at me long enough for me to see that he might play a part in his brother's decision. For a second I see the dimensions and chipped paint of the closet that he has decided to live in.

–Thanks Joe.

Here, on the ground next to my four slashed tyres and my four new ones ready for a spin on rural roads, I have been thinking about the woman I fell in love with while I was running from her and I have let her go.

March comes in like a lion roaring from the sky. Midwestern spring rain comes down like a west of Scotland wet rage. When I wake up at three to the smell of her skin again, the rain has stopped but the night is raincloud dark. I get dressed, shorts and then trousers on top. I put on a University of Wisconsin sweatshirt that one of my students gave me, and my light waterproof.

The air is heavy and I start walking to get myself used to the change of season. When I begin to run I close my eyes for all the difference it makes to what I am able to see. Above my breathing and the sound of my feet on the track, I hear the rattling of the fence and then waiting.

I don't know how she managed it, but I smell heather. Through the rain air, through the dark, I smell heather and as I continue to run my heart resists the urge to pound. There are strides beside me. Hard breathing. Lungs unused to night running strain beside me. I let them. After awhile I feel a strong hand on my forearm, she pulls me still.

The track is rough but the grass softer and very wet. We could be arrested for what we do together as we move between the two, not really caring if the ground beneath us gives way completely. Later we sit on the cold aluminium stands and watch the sun rise.

–I've got a joke for you. She pokes my shoulder and

encourages me to look excited. I nudge her back urging her to tell it. –It's about Jesus and Satan having a contest to prove who can do more with their computer. God is there to judge the winner. They have two hours. They sit at their keyboards, hands flying. They mouse, they do spreadsheets and graphs, reports and databases. They fax and they email. A few minutes short of two hours the power goes out and the computer screens go blank. Satan curses and damns, 'I've lost everything.' The screens come back on and Jesus pushes print and all of his work is there. 'How did he do that?' Satan asks God. God smiles, 'Jesus Saves.'

I laugh, impressed. Context matters. Where I saw hatred plastered on the back of a Chevy; she saw a prison of beliefs and turned it into humour. When I ran my finger along the cool black interior of the empty envelope I saw rejection where I should have seen her struggle to find the words for the truth she knew.

Thinking of the back of a Toyota with four new tyres Anna asks me, –So when do we go out in the boat? She smiles, breathing in the night and exhaling the dawn, and I know that no one in their right or wrong mind could make her anything but what she is. And for now, for a while, she is mine and she is here. Her cold hand takes my own and she leads me back to the apartment knowing that she is no recruit.

The Café at the End of the World

Jen Hadfield

The tourists keep coming as late as September. The mountain road is still open. As long as Applecross is passable it's still summer. Summer, the mountain road: they're like everything here. Stretched and splinted open as far as possible, before the white slopes clamp shut about the tarmac like a kicked limpet. The hairpins zagging towards the bay are something from a Bond film. Sandstone scree rubbles under the black and white barriers, as if stuffing is being knocked out of the mountain. I've picked up pieces of lore about it. Unspoken rules. Give way to uphill traffic. Never stop to take snaps from the passing places. You have to keep an eye on a mountain like Applecross.

Reviewers in travel books have described the bay as a Western frontier. So we have two names on the sign out front: 'Kishorn Seafood and Snackbar' and 'Bar Blasad Bidhe Agus Biadh Na Mara.' Sometimes our customers try and do the Gaelic. I used to laugh at them, but couldn't pronounce it myself. And now I always call it 'The Café at the End of the World', as Ole dubbed it.

When I arrived the sky was grey, doubtful. It was a long way to have come, hitching. I felt around the top of my pack for the roll I picked up at a roadside café. It was soggy in its own steam but I hadn't liked to eat in the last car I was in, a vacuumed people-carrier that stopped for me in Glen Shiel. Before I'd even got the plastic bag from round it there were gulls everywhere, mean things, size of albatrosses. I was doing this hop-skipping thing on the spot. Then this giant was suddenly out of one of the cottages, and bellowing 'Jul!' and a hound flew from his ankles at the gulls. I didn't even have the click of a latch to warn me.

'Half terrier, half collie, half devil, he's a dog and a half, eh, Jul?'

The dog was at the guy's feet. 'Come on, you can leave your pack there, I'll give you tea. Bring your roll. You can't listen to those meanies if you want to eat.'

'And where are you running from?' he said, filling up a disappointedly modern cordless kettle. 'It was Norway for me,' (which explained the accent) 'though that was ten years ago, and I'm thinking, though ten years goes quicker at my age than yours, it might be time for me to take off again...'

'Take off?' I should've been narked. But he was telling his past and it could've been my own. Being brought up a believer of modern myths. The training, the sensible job, where you meet the partner you know is sensible, by the fact people refer to them as your partner. (The city was where my nark was currently residing, alive and well.) And then this sudden lust for road movies and Kerouac, until you realise. What you actually need to be doing is *living* a road movie. You ask the partner for a rucksack for Christmas, and when they buy you one of those handbag-haversacks you're unsurprised, appalled, decided. You jack it all in for a one-way rail ticket. Or in Ole's case, a bunk-less fare to Lerwick, Stromness, and Scrabster.

'Actually I hate the sea. My father was so turned on by all that continental shelf business, I was still scared of falling off it,' Ole said.

I didn't have to ask why he still lived on the sea, working with the engines of trawlers. I had the same thing with mountains.

Fucking terrified of them, the vertigo, the rock falls, the exposure, the blasted hugeness of boulder fields. You have to make sure you're constantly surrounded by your fears, just to scupper fate. You've got to give your fear a good hard stare every day, keep it where it belongs. As for Ole, I could tell by the angle of his foot reflecting mine, his arm flat on the formica. He even gripped his mug like me, looking doubtfully into it. You know your doubles when you meet them. I knew the moment my belly stopped singing the phobia song. It had started small with the bumpy babyhills of Lower Tyndrum, swelling through Rannoch, Glencoe and peaking at Applecross, *keep moving keep moving s'alright it's OK, it's alright.* Now it stopped and my guts just said, quiet as a latch unlocking, *yes.*

And Ole opened Kishorn for me. When he introduced me to Mairie I got work at the seafood café, and unlike the summer workers, stayed. We have oysters, squats, crevettes, squid, clams, scallops I've learned to call queenies, crabs thick as discuses. In summer the day's catch sells out by two, but we never lock the door. There's still tea, even chowder, and if all else fails, good white rolls. We sell ourselves out to the last cold curl of butter. There's a special blade for shucking oysters. If you don't know exactly where to cranny it in, the shell crumbles in white flakes. Or the blade slips and punctures the oyster. I've always made a mess of them.

Now the autumn's coming. The gales haven't started yet, but already the stilts are shoogley. The birches are whipping. And still folk will wait two hours to sit at tables overlooking the bay, watch fishing boats prowl the sheltered water like mousers. Once tired of being harassed by gulls, they take four-wheel-drives down the track to the village, sit and watch the sunset. They're fascinated by the same things that used to fascinate me. Creels, squashed orange buoys. They're startled by water that's so clear they can see crabs knitting the seaweed, doing that *tai chi* bit under the rotting jetty. They peer into locals' gardens through netting that protects vegetables from the wind. Poke stinking heaps of seaweed till the sandhoppers leap. In the mats of thrift, around the irises, are green sea urchins. The photos, back in the cities, will look like they were taken with filters – sun stained. The shots taken from Applecross' lay-bys make Kishorn look very small.

Occasionally a visitor gets carried away with visions of the beach hut and barbecue life. That was Gordon two years ago. He sat around on his five rocks till he realised no one was about to make a film, and finally headed to the bar like everybody else. That's where Mairie is now. She will have served the last cups of tourist tea and the first of the pints – to Gordon, quiet Angus, and maybe Jamie. First time I went along it was because Mairie said I could, but I went mainly because I was bound to meet Ole there. Sure enough, I found them lined up at the counter, gossiping about fish farming. Ole was talking it up, explaining to Angus about a type of net that Angus had made up, it didn't even exist.

He's going, 'There's a leader from the shore, it runs out into two wings…' All this with those Norwegian vowels spreading like oil spill. I edge into the conversation, get a wink. Happiness is cider and the bright pineapples and cherries on the fruit machine. Then Mairie butts in about the latest casualties.

'In Maree,' she says, 'Lorna's son's son, no, not *Alfie*, Alfie's *son*.'

'Was he not drunk all the time?' slurs Ole gorgeously, leaning into her voice, and I've got a jealous pang in my belly.

'No, now listen, that was Alfie, always a couple cans before breakfast. Just to settle himself. You get to that point. No. It was something caught round the prop and he went down and never came back up… that was it. No. I'm wrong, it was off Raasay.'

Angus says, 'I've never been on Raasay,' and Gordon says,

'God, have I been somewhere you haven't?' And Angus says,

'Aye, Raasay. No. I went once. Sheep on the rocks,' and he puts out his hand for his pint.

Two months. Still word for word. Just as well. *Two months*, and Mairie still lets me off the shucking. Yeh, it was the 18th of July. Near closing. I washed the floor, sluiced the ice trays. Then I took the last three oysters and a half scoop of steamed squats outside. I looked over the bay and the boats turning slowly round their anchors. I was feeling weird, happy I thought, no need to stare at mountains today. The first oyster I ever opened cleanly. Weaselled the blade in, gave a sharp turn to the left. As the shell eased open, winched tight with muscle, Mairie's white van pulled up. I smiled at her, holding up the oyster, she smiled back. Something funny with her face.

She said, 'He was on his way back from Sildvik.' I was confused and put down the shell and the shucker.

'What?' There were gulls, all about me.

'He was on his way back with an engine. Nearly home. Helping someone out with an engine, and his own fucking brake gives in,' I thought she was joking, but then the gulls were yelping and she was shaking. I couldn't work out what she was talking about, but out of habit looked up to Applecross. The barrier looked odd. There was a red speck jammed in the gully. My palm stopped mid-circle on her back. I'd forgotten my fingers were shelly with squat lobster. The gulls angled, I couldn't feel to flinch. My skin snipped deep, cleanly for a moment, then the blood started stinging out and running over, and this weird butterflies dread was whammelling in my stomach and I started to see something had happened and there was nowhere I could take off to that would ever make me feel normal again.

Odd all my settling down should've happened from that point. Even walking to the bar in the dark, in the big shadowy black of mountain and sky and water, there's no need to look. Settling down has mainly meant my own seat at the counter, and Jul's head on the low rung of my stool. Sometimes swithering home, with dawn coming, is difficult. The gulls are dreamier then, pure white bellies against a lightening sky. *Geal.* Best to cover your ears. I'm not scared. But it could make you cry, the seagulls moaning.

Drawing Water

Ingrid Lees

It has got worse for me over the last few weeks. Much worse. The rejection – being pushed out of the way again and again, shooed to the back of the cluster of grown girls, with their jerrycans at the well; my peer group, who I am so desperate to be part of, and know for sure I never shall. In spite of us all having the blue-black Acholi[1] skin under the merciless sun, my sheer presence is resented. I'm wished away, away for ever. I'm used to it. But it has never been as bad as this. Before. I have always managed to get water at the well, eventually, after the others had got all they wanted.

But now in the drought the water is very low. The well has almost run dry. Our cows are starting to die. All of us Acholi people are thin, as not much food is left in the granaries, and what is left has to last until the new crops are ready. But we can't even sow and plant because there is no rain and the ground is baked hard. Covered in red dust we look up at the sky for the signs of rain. But there are none. We chant for rain and make offerings. But there is no answer. We pray in our mud church to the White God. But he seems not to hear either. The little water there is cannot be wasted. Now it is getting so bad that the other girls resent even a drop of water used by me. They don't let me get near the well.

'Get away with your buckled jerrycan. You will only spill the precious water,' they say, chase me like a hen and expect me to do without. Without water, shrivelling under the blazing sun when I am expected to bring back water to my compound.

I wish that I, Akello[2], the first-born twin girl, could change

[1] The Acholi people live in northern Uganda.
[2] Akello is the name given to a first-born twin girl.

place with my twin sister, whose name stayed empty at birth, who is left in peace in her burial place under the ancient holy tree of our ancestors. But I, the privileged first-born, have to swing my body and the skeletal folded locust legs with my arms on the wooden blocks to get around, cannot walk, run or dance. I am condemned to a joyless existence. Laughed at and written off. Called *Locust without a Jump*, when in fact I am healthy and strong but for the polio legs. My heart is aching and my breasts tingle, wanting to be stroked and sucked by a baby. But it is not to be. The girls laugh and the boys look the other way as if I didn't exist, were invisible. Occasionally Omolo, who was the clever one at school with us, looks at me fleetingly with kind eyes when his friends and the other girls aren't looking. Or am I imagining this to console myself? At least he is not laughing at me like the others.

The girls around the well let the bucket down again and again. Its emptiness comes up easily, swinging from side to side. Only a few cups of muddy brown liquid are gained each time. Water thick and precious. And none of it for me.

With parched lips I swing myself nearer to the cluster of girls. Maybe this time they will take pity and let me have a little for my jerrycan.

'Get away, you monstrous locust, there isn't enough. It's running out,' they shout and swing their arms at me to chase me off.

Tears well up in my eyes and a lump rises into my throat. I turn away from the group. The jerrycan with its hollow clank and the half calabash[3] strapped to my back are my shadow.

Painfully I follow the narrow path through the bush. The tall

[3] A dried gourd used as ladle, cup, container, as a sunshade for a baby's head when carried on the back.

elephant grass is closed over at the top. I concentrate fully on the physical effort to stop my tears, to push the lump in my throat down again and bear my heavy heart.

Thrust weight and wooden blocks forward,
swing body with the folded legs
Thrust weight and wooden blocks forward,
swing body with the folded legs
Thrust weight and wooden blocks forward,
swing body with the folded legs

On and on along the winding elephant grass tunnel. My heart is aching and my mind stunned, but my body is strong. I'm good at this swinging. Well practiced. Have made my way through the bush to school every day like this, three long miles there and three long miles back. Always got there and back home. Was good at reading and writing and the sums, can sing all the songs and tell the stories of my people. But what is the good of it without the dancing? Can make a fire, but not gather the wood. Can cook, wash clothes and smear the floor with mud, but the walls only halfway up. Can grow food in the shamba[4] and sweep the compound with a short broom. But I cannot stand up and look dignified. Beside my people in my homestead nobody wants to look at me. They seem ashamed to look and see. Don't know what to say.

After four long parched miles of swinging I find myself down at the dried up river bed. Our lovely river of plenty now turned into a valley of sand. I make my way carefully down the river bank and pull myself through the loose sand. I unstrap the jerry can and calabash, useless without water, and start digging with my bare hands scooping up the sand and flinging it behind me to both sides. As the hole is deepening, for quickness and to

[4] garden, field

save my hands, I now use the calabash for digging sand, my calabash that ought to be used for bailing water into my jerry can. But the dry sand collapses in again and again. I dig faster and faster, work myself into a mad frenzy, fired by the injustice. All I can do does not count. Only what I can't do matters and stops me from everything.

I'm digging on and on, though I don't know what I'm digging for. There is no hope of water in this dry sand. As the hole deepens I have to haul myself down into it to continue. There is shade down here. It protects me from the sun, still hot but getting low now. Soon it will be dark. I dig on thinking of my twin sister, who I could never know, down in her resting place under the holy ancestral tree. Someone must have dug a hole for her. And now I am digging a hole for myself in the river bed. Here I can hide with my useless locust legs that refuse to walk and dance. Here I can find peace. Sweat stands in my face and trickles down my back. I dig on obsessed. I cannot stop myself. Have to go on digging my hole. It is deep now. I don't know whether I can crawl out again. But that doesn't matter as I don't want to crawl out. This is my hole. Let it be deep enough so I can hide and don't have to face the humiliation any longer. My safe hole.

I am burning hot, yet have stopped sweating. There is no sweat left. My mouth is parched, my thirst terrible. Tears want to rise into my sore dry eyes rubbed by sand grains. But there are no tears left. I am crying and sobbing without tears. My body is drying up. I can hardly see what I am doing but continue the rhythm of digging. My strong body is tiring, my mind muddled. In front of my eyes appear legs. Straight and strong, they start dancing. I crouch amongst them, have to save myself from being trodden on. And they dance and dance to the drumming, faster and faster, these straight strong Acholi legs so unlike mine. Voices sound all around laughing, mocking and jeering. The more they jeer and the faster they dance, the faster I dig keeping up with the drumming in my head. Some white holy man shouts again and again, 'Get up and rise.'

All the dancers point at me, laugh and jeer, 'She can't, locust, she can't, locust...'

And they all whirl around me faster and faster while I keep digging in a mad fury to the beat of the drums.

The sand in the calabash feels very heavy in my tired arms and I have to fling it very high up by now. But I keep going to the rhythm of the drums.

Then in the fading light my dry grated eyes see something glinting right down at the bottom of my hole. With my sandy arms I clumsily rub my eyes to see what this is. Looks like dampness. Maybe tears. Yet my eyes are dry and sore. Could it be sweet water? Then deeper down there would be more. I dig faster and faster and see water. Very little. But water. With my fingers I rub some on my lips and taste it. It is not salty tears, but earthy water. I carefully scoop as much as I can into my calabash, put it to my lips and drink with my dried-out mouth.

As soon as more water has seeped into the hole I scoop up more with the calabash and raise it with my tired arms to the darkening sky to give thanks to the ancestors, the River God and the White God. As I see the darkening sky above, a shout of relief leaves my sobbing throat. In the frenzy of dancing legs, mocking voices, skeletons of ancestors, gods and the drumming in my head, I am looking into two eyes. Astonished kind eyes in the fading light.

Entertaining Visitors

Rena McEwan

There they were, sitting on my windowsill looking in at me. Two great big crows. Their beady eyes never left me. They sat there, as though waiting for me to do something to make them laugh. I was the chosen entertainment. There was nothing I could do about it, because I had taken down the ghastly venetian blind the day before. Meaning to replace it with something a bit more aesthetically pleasing. Only, today I had allowed myself to be sidetracked into starting my novel, and of course as any experienced novelist will tell you, once you are 'in the flow' time simply flies. And now it was dark winter evening, and these two crows were making their home on my windowsill.

I saw them look at my big green couch, then my blue sofa bed. And heard them cackle like banshees. Then they turned their eyes on me. They watched every move I made. I began to feel nervous, drop things, trip over the rug. Each time they cackled even more, as though I was confirming some inner prejudice of theirs. Then they would look at each other and make throaty noises of communication. And I thought, They're talking about me!

I turned my back on them, tried to ignore them. I was hungry and began preparing something to eat. I'll do stir fry, I thought, and took out my teflon-coated wok. Cackle, cackle! I looked at my wok. 'Alright!' I yelled at them, 'I'm planning to buy a better one soon!'

Silence. I took some vegetables from the fridge, and a bit of chicken breast. The croaking and flapping of wings was deafening. I put the chicken breast back. I brought out some basmati rice and measured out three ounces in the cup. Cackles of derision. I became clumsy, spilled the rice on to the floor, had to sweep it up and bin it. More cackles, this time gleeful. I began to sweat.

I finally managed to get the rice cooking, and the vegetables sliced and into the hot wok. A dash of wine, I thought, a touch of L&P and some black bean sauce. With just a hint of ginger. But my hand was slippy with sweat when I poured the wine, which was cold from the fridge. Too much wine, and the wok cooled down, leaving the vegetables marinading rather than cooking. Then the top came off the Lea & Perrins and a dash turned into half the bottle. Cackle, cackle, cackle, cackle. I lost my appetite.

This can't go on, I thought. I'll phone a friend. I picked up my cordless telephone and dialed Rebecca's number. But the noise from my windowsill became so deafening I had to hang up. By now I was close to tears. Rage, I told myself. Frustration. But my breathing began to change, become shallow. An overwhelming feeling of helplessness. Then a wave of something, fear, that started in my gut and began to work upwards. I knew that as soon as it reached my brain I was finished. I reached for something big and heavy, and my hand found the old fire iron that had belonged to my granny. With all the remaining strength I had I threw it at the window. The glass shattered, the crows squawked and flew off in panic, and the cold north wind entered my bedsit and made itself comfortable.

The Great Divide

Margaret Mansell

Saturday Morning

Slumped in a comfy green tartan chair, Kimberley looks at the television and lifting the control, channel hops until she finds the news. Cautiously she sips hot black liquid from an emerald cup. She takes two tablets from the boxes on the pine table and swallowing these she chokes and splutters coffee down the front of her dressing gown. Sighing she mops at the damp patches. Propping her feet on a round footstool, she contemplates her perfectly painted jade toenails.

The telephone rings interrupting the tranquility. Shaking her head she grabs up the receiver.

'Hello?' she answers hoarsely, pulling the earpiece away from her ear.

The voice on the other end booms, 'Hi Kimberley hen, it's me, Coreen. God ye sound awful. Whit's wrang?'

'Hi Coreen, ah've goat a chist infection. A don't feel well,' she replies coughing.

'Aw, that's nae good. Hiv ye goat anythin tae take?' asks her friend sympathetically.

'Aye, antibiotics fae the doaktor. He sent me tae the Vicky fur a chist x-ray, an Ah've tae go back next week fur the results. But Ah'll be aw right afore then,' she replies bravely.

Changing the subject Coreen says, 'Kim, mind A mentioned that barbecue tae ye a couple o weeks ago? A don't suppose ye feel up to it noo dae ye? It's the night, at ma pal Elaine's brother's hoose, in South Park Village. Jist alang the road fae you.' Speaking faster now she continues, 'Eh's name's

Paul. Eh's a bity a lad. Ye've goat tae watch him! Eh's goat a bird. But eh's bin talkin aboot binnin hur fur ages, an you're jist his type,' she warns her friend.

Suddenly feeling much better, Kimberley answers, 'Aw Coreen, A forgoat aw aboot it. But, aye, A'll go. It'll help take ma mind aff things.'

'Ur ye sure?' asks a concerned Coreen.

'Aye, it'll dae me the world o good,' says Kimberley determinedly.

'Brilliant. Aye Kim, it probably wull dae ye good. A get tae the Pollok Centre aboot haulf six. Kin ye pick me up?' she asks hopefully.

'Aye, sure. A'll get you at haulf six. We'll lea the motur here and walk oer. Then A kin hiv a wee swallay tae,' she answers enthusiastically.

'Great. See ye efter. Bye Kim'.

'Bye, Coreen,' croaks Kimberley.

Preparation

Clunking down the earpiece Kimberley springs quickly out of her chair. Sprinting upstairs she tugs eagerly at the gold handled doors of the ivory wardrobe. Garments are scattered over the floor as she rummages for the perfect outfit. She delightedly lays her selection on the bed. In the bathroom she pours lime green essences into the frothing hot and cold water. Inching her aching body into the warm bubbles, she relaxes before the rest of the house awakes.

After a long day of household chores and entertaining her offspring, she is ready. Short dark hair perfect, she's dressed to thrill in tight blue jeans, olive belly-revealing top and black sandals. Her make up is carefully applied, hiding pale complexion, red nose and dark shadows below the eyes.

Ready, eager and willing to P-A-R-T-Y, she calls to her sons, 'Bowys, am goan tae pick up Coreen fae the Centre.'

Leaning over the timber banister, spectacled, flame-haired Brad, wearing Radiohead T-shirt and baggy ink-black jeans, shouts back, 'OK, ma. See ye later.'

Tall, dark-haired Robbie in Sainsbury's uniform emerges from his bedroom, leaving raucous nightclub behind. Aftershave fumes waft around, filling the hallway with a delicious scent. Pausing he asks, 'Whit did ye say ma? Wheer ur ye goan?'

Eyes raised, she answers, 'Remembur, A told ye, Pollok Centre. Tae pick up Coreen. Wur goan tae a partey. A'll bring the motur back here furst. See ye efter.'

He turns back towards his disco inferno and shouts over his shoulder, 'Aw right Ma. Cheerio.'

The thunder of feet approach, then shouts of, 'Mammy, mammy.'

'Mammy' stands, hand outstretched towards the front door and sighing asks, 'Whit Tyrone?'

Adoringly he tilts his small grubby face to one side and asks hopefully, 'Kin yea bring me back sum sweeties fae the shoaps?'

Patiently she answers, 'Naw the shoaps are shut noo. A'm goan tae pick up Aunty Coreen. We're goan tae a partey.'

'Kin A cum tae the partey?'

'Naw sun, it's for big yins. Yer too wee. Brad will watch ye.'

'Aw right then mammy. Bye-bye.' He waves a chubby hand and clambers back up the stairs to play with his games console.

'Bye, babe,' she affectionately calls after the retreating figure.

Pick Up

Kimberley picks up Coreen and they swap the gossip as she drives at speed along Peat Road in her battered pillar-box red Ford Cortina.

'Kimberley dae yea waant tae chip in fur a bowtle o' cider and some cans fur the partey?' asks Coreen hopefully.

'Aw, sorry Coreen. A canny, am skint this week. A thought add jist take that bowtle o wine A've goat in the fridge,' she apologises.

'That's aw right, never mind. Bowtle o wine! Oh A wish A'd bowt wan,' she coaxes.

'Dae ye waant me tae drive ye tae the shoaps tae get wan?' asks Kimberley.

'Sure you widnay mind?' answers Coreen in mock surprise. 'Am such a pest.'

'Naw, course A don't mind,' she replies.

They pick up a select bottle of wine and some cans of beer from the shops. Back at the house they deposit the car, issue safety warnings to the offspring and kiss them 'bye' for now.

On The Way

The evening is warm and the girls continue their journey on foot. They stroll down idyllic sweet-smelling, country lanes before turning into South Park Village. As they merrily wander along Coreen inquires of her friend, 'Wheer ur we goan Kimberley?'

Confused, Kimberley answers, 'Whit dae ye mean, wheer ur we goan? You should know wheer wur goan. A've never bin tae

Paul's hoose afore. You said ye kid see Sainsbury's fae his back gerden. But, A don't think ye kin see Sainsbury's fae any o the gerdens in this estate! Whit's eh's address?' She's snippy now.

They stop to rest, dumping their heavy plastic carrier bags on the pavement. Coreen holds out a hand and looking at the ink-smudged sweaty palm, tries to decipher what she'd written a few hours ago. 'It's, eh. It's. A think it's 19 somethin way. But, it's oan a piece o' paper in ma bag. Wait!' She fiddles about in her handbag and finding a smaller bag, she gropes inside this unsuccessfully. Searching the pockets of her jacket she mumbles to herself, 'Am such a plank. Oh, ma God, no again. A always screw up the arrangements.'

Looking at Kimberley's glowering face she asks hopefully, 'D'ye think anybidy roun here wid hiv a list o street names?'

'Naw Coreen, A don't. The only wan who'd hive a list wid be a taxi driver,' she answers. 'Yer a numpty! See if ye kin spot a taxi.'

Shaking her head, Coreen says, 'Aw, A canny believe me, whit a Wally. Look, is that a taxi? Aw naw, it's jist a cor.'

'Coreen, hiv ye goat Elaine's brother's phone number?' sighs Kimberley resignedly.

'Naw, but A know Elaine's number and someday'll be there watching her weans. They'll gie us the number.'

'Whit is it then? A've got ma phone in ma bag.'

'It's, ehm, it's. Oh Kim A'm sorry A canny remembur. It's 0141-636, or is it 403 – and a canny remembur the rest,' she apologises sheepishly.

'Coreen! Let's jist walk up here. If we walk tae the other side o the estate, where B&Q is, mibbe ye kin see Sainsbury's fae they back gerdens. Aw right?' she suggests hopefully.

'Oh, ma feet are killing me in these shoes and A'm sweatin like a pig. Somedy here must know where there's a place ending in 'way' roun here,' she bleats.

Through gritted teeth Kimberley replies, 'Jist keep walkin!'

Heavy bags in hand, they totter round the streets, like Billy Connolly's joke about the drunk lugging his *'cairy oot'* on New Year's Eve, walking round listening for sounds of a party to join – any party! They spot a cheery assortment of green and white-hooped youths on a corner, some leaning against the lamppost, some sitting on the pavement.

'A'll ask these bowys if they know where 19 something way is,' says Coreen cheerfully.

'Naw, Cor don't ask them, they will'ny know,' says a horrified Kimberley. 'Yer such a brass neck.'

Fascinated, the boys stare wide-eyed at the approaching figure, with flowing red hair, dressed in black Capri pants, tight white blouse and blood-red high heels.

'Chaps, any you know where we can find a place endin in way roun here? We're invited tae a party at ma mate Elaine's brother's hoose. He lives at 19 something way.'

Smirking they eye each other in amazement and enthusiastically shoot questions at the two bizarre women,

Hiv you goat the guy's phone number?

'Eh, naw, a canny remembur it,' apologises an embarrassed Coreen.

Whit's the guy's name then?

'It's Paul,' she continues.

Paul whit?

'A don't know, it's eh's sister A know really.'

Whit's the sister's name then?

'Elaine,' she answers brightly.

Elaine whit?

'A, ehm, a canny remembur!'

Howls of laughter fill the air and a mortified Kimberley wanders off muttering to herself. The boys hold on to their sides or throw their arms around each other to stop falling over. Immensely enjoying the situation they direct non-stop questions at the bewildered Coreen.

Ur ye sure it's South Park Village ye waant?

Mibbe ye waant Park House Estate,

Ur Darnley, mibbe ye waant Darnley,

Ur Priesthill,

Ur Arden,

Ur South Nitshill,

Ur!

'Aright bowys thanks anywie,' replies the humiliated Coreen.

With the boy's laughter and taunts reverberating in her ears she sidles off in search of Kimberley, who is impatiently waiting at the next corner.

'Kimberley, whits rang wi ye? Ye'v goat a coupin like a wet weekend. It's aw right noo, A've jist rememburd. It's 19 Oakleaf Way.'

'Ur ye sure that's in South Park, Coreen?' inquires Kimberley doubtfully.

'Aye, a think so. The taxi driver mentioned South Park Village the last time.'

Impatiently she asks, 'Eh didnae say somethin like, that's South Park Village oer there. Ur,up the road. Ur, in the next toon. Did eh?'

Coreen's face flushes as red as her shoes as she answers, 'A canny remembur. Oh, d'ye think it's no here efter aw?' Decisively she orders, 'Kimberley, git oot yer mobey an phone is a taxi. The taxi driver'll find it.'

'Aw right then. Whit's the number?'

'It's ehm. It's – 0141-880-3403.'

Kimberley quickly presses the numbers on the keypad of her mobile telephone, 'Kin a hiv a taxi please? Whit? Phhhhhh! Aw, don't bother then, thanks anywie! Coreen they canny get us wan for forty minutes. We're as well to keep walkin.'

'Keep walkin? Ma dogs are barking! Am no wandrin roun an roun in circles,' moans Coreen. She plonks her ample backside on the brick wall of an adjacent garden.

'Well, A'll ask this young couple if they know wheer it is,' says Kimberley hopefully as she quickly walks off.

'Aw right, A'll ask this man up here,' replies Coreen, reluctantly climbing down from the comfort of her brick seat.

Both meet up once again at the corner with the news update that 19 Oakleaf way is in fact in Darnley – a twenty-minute walk away, in the estate across the road!

Groaning and eyeing her 'poor' feet Coreen said contritely, 'Sorry Kim, a thowt it was here.'

'Cor, yi're such a plonker. Yid forgit yer heid if it wisnay screwed oan. Right we know wheer wur goan noo. Cum oan.'

'Aw, A wish A'd put oan ma auld flat shoes, insteid o these stupit high heels,' whines Coreen.

Success

Twenty minutes later the bedraggled beauties shuffle wearily but gratefully up the path of 19 Oakleaf Way. Approaching they hear loud music. They walk through the house and into the back garden where the music centre blasts out Irish ballads. The girls stop as they face the sea of green and white. Tricolour flags, streamers and balloons are hung along the wall and fences. Inebriated green-and-white shirted men and women raise cans of lager to toast *Celtic, the Pope* and *the IRA* and in defiance stick two fingers in the air, calling *the Queen* and *the Huns*.

Kimberley, the interloping Protestant Rangers supporter turns to her good Catholic friend and inquires, '*Coreen, whit's this?*'

'Aw, Kim did a no tell yea. Celtic and Hibs wur playin fur the cup the day and Celtic won. The barbecue's a celebration. Yea don't mind, dae yea?'

Freaks

Nick Brooks

Tell ye the place was full of freaks man. There was no seats left thegither, we were that late getting on board so we both sat where we could. One at the front one at the back. It was near full: Friday night, all the folk coming back up for the weekend. They already had the dimmer lights on and half the curtains were drawn over and I just bumped myself over all these invisible limbs. Squeezed in next to some geezer who was kidding on he was asleep, his head turned in at the window. No idea who'd nabbed the seats. I was ragin cause we had them booked and everything. It wisnae as if we just turned up cold, though I was needing my jacket and it was in wi the luggage. The driver says if he got any trouble off us he was gonnae just chip us off, didnae matter where we were, he was just gonnae chip us off on the hard shoulder and that would be that. We could hitch it back for aw he cared. We werenae after any trouble we says, we widnae be any bother, he widnae even notice us there. I was gonnae be up at the lav every ten minutes but. I knew that. What d'ye make of that I says to the geezer next to me. He wisnae gonnae let us board – says we've drank too much! Fuckin nightmare man. London bus drivers eh. Fucking Mexicans and all that.

The geezer gave us a shock but – I had to check myself. He must have got burnt sometime – he was all raw, the skin of his lips stretched tight across his face, all the lines smoothed away like he was ageless. He had hair starting at the edge of it. He looked like a fuckin jigsaw man. A fuckin scare he gave us. I couldnae think of anything to say to him. I was stuck, looking at his face. There was nowhere else for me to go. I'm like, starting to get panicky, the microdot kicking in. The sweats. This geezer, he was jumpy as anything n I just started running off at the mouth to cover myself, every word coming out wrong. I'm like, Sorry man I just meant... what I was meaning was... blah blah blah... couldnae stop myself. A closed groove man. The bus hadnae even got going yet. On the lighter fuel were ye? I says. I was sorry as soon as I opened my gub. He could see I wisnae going to gie him any peace so he got up and went for a different seat. I was glad in a way and sorry in another. I was digging my own grave there for a while. For the next eight hour I must have just stared out the windae. I didnae even bother with the lav till we were smuggled safe north of the border.

What can I tell ye? The girlfriend and me split when we got off. The end. We'd went and stuck the bags in the other bus and had to wait for it to come in to the station, and we're like shivering away, me still shirted up Hawaiian style. Then the ex-girlfriend turns on the waterworks. Try stayin sober, the driver says. Mibby yis'll have better luck. But she'd had about enough, we were two different people and all that. She went off and left me wi nowt but pesetas in my back pocket. Blah blah blah. There was no sense in it. I'm just like, standing there, watching these birds swoop about above the bus station. Hundreds of them, this dull recycled light coming up and the streets wet wi nobody on them. Only black whirring dots, sparrows or something, throwing this mad semaphore up against the sky. I just stood there watching. I was trying to understand it, get my head around what they were trying to say. Then I started walking. Someone asked us for change. It might have been Coco the Clown, but that was just the chef's outfit. The whites and the chequered trousers. He was missing the warpaint. Split a taxi wi ye? I says. He was a bit on the slow side. I had to say it again... Tonto no want to get heap big taxi, *sabe?* We were going the same way and everything but he just looks and says:

Ye can get the jail for that.

I couldnae believe it. We were both standing in a fucking bus shelter to get out the rain at six in the fuckin morning, fuck all between us or anything – blah blah blah. He needs a taxi, I need a taxi and he's givin me this shite about the jail! Talking different fucking languages man. It was pishing down but I starts walking anyway. Just to get away again. Then I turned and goes –

Tonto mibby get lucky if he get um heap big red nose out!

Home on the range again man. Where the queer and the antelope play. Nightmare.

Fun and Furore

Lois Brooks

Is it the light in this bathroom or do I really look such a wreck? Goodness gracious, I've aged ten years in as many hours. My eyes are as puffy as two fried eggs. How can he put me through such humiliation? I could never do this to someone I loved. But then I'm not a pervert. And I have to face it, that's what Jeffrey is. My own son, a pervert.

It seems so out of character, people have always said what a nice gentle sort Jeffrey is. Heavens above, he was a Scout leader till he went away to college. He comes for dinner every Wednesday and I make him lasagne or chicken curry, his favourites. And I've always got a supply of chocolate-covered Hobnobs to have with a cuppa when it's time for *Coronation Street*. Of course, for the past few months he's been bringing along that witch Deborah with her dyed black hair. I always thought it looked so unnatural on a young girl. Now I know she *is* unnatural, they both are. She's got a face like a pin cushion; pierced ears, pierced nose, pierced eyebrows and – she thought I hadn't noticed but not much escapes me – there's a ball bearing sort of thing dangling around on her tongue. But you know, truth be told, Deborah's been very kind to me. Painted my living room and kitchen during the Christmas break and, when I twisted my ankle in the snow, she was over three or four times a week doing my shopping and housework. We'd sit and watch *Wheel of Fortune* over a cuppa. She told me how Jeffrey was working hard on their business plan and – good grief, I could kick myself now – I never asked her any more about it because, to be frank, I can't stand her Liverpool accent. I had to give up

Brookside because of the way they all talk. Anyway, I assumed this 'business' they were planning was to sell the arts and crafts stuff they made at college, jewellery and the likes. The presents they gave me at Christmas, they'd made all by themselves. Silver hoop earrings from Jeffrey – for pierced ears and I wear clip-ons. I thought at the time, typical, men, they never notice the finer details. I got a black leather belt from madam, hardly my style but I thanked her all the same. All covered in studs and things. I chopped a bit off the length and handed it in to Mrs McDougall to use as a collar for Rory, her Alsatian dog.

I still can't believe what Jeffrey's gone and done. It feels like a bad dream. You know, in normal circumstances I'm loath to phone in sick – you get so much of it on the wards – but this morning I had to. I phoned in stunned. Staff Nurse Duddie took the call and when I said I wouldn't manage my back shift, I'd come down with a nasty virus, she said, 'Well, take care. We're all thinking about you.' Thinking about me, indeed! I could hear the sniggers in the background. Good Lord, it doesn't bear thinking about! They all read that paper, flick through it at breaktime. Truth be told, I've scoffed and tut-tutted along with them at the smut and sleaze in the tabloids. Good heavens, how will I ever face going back to work? How will I ever face the neighbours? How will I face anyone, anywhere?

All day I've asked myself, is it my fault, is it something I did wrong? They say these weird things are linked to childhood experiences. But Jeffrey showed no signs of being… odd. Now if he was gay or something, I could handle that. At least I think I could. It's very PC to be gay these days. Nurse Johnson's son's gay and you'd never guess. Nice, polite, young man. Not effeminate in the least, but then, neither was Rock Hudson. Goodness gracious, if Jeffrey's father were alive today he'd absolutely murder him. You know, we smacked Jeffrey when he was little, only when he was very naughty, mind. Maybe that's what this is all about, a rebellion against being smacked. But, no, that's ridiculous. Everyone got smacked back then. What I hate most is the fool he's made of me! Why did he make *my* name public? Why didn't he make his own name public – especially now that he's picked himself a new one! He doesn't seem to care, he's loving it, going right ahead with more of the same and worse… Doesn't he realise how all this affects me?

I keep seeing that photograph, can't get it out my head. There I was, sitting with my paper, my mid-morning cuppa, a couple of Hobnobs, turned the page and, good Lord in heaven, I nearly took a backwards tumble out of my chair! There was no mistaking them, Jeffrey and Deborah posing inside what looked like a dungeon! Deborah, or should I say 'Brittney Pierce', has got my Jeffrey, or should I say 'Whipme Houston', attached to a lead! And round his neck he's wearing a studded dog collar just like the one I gave Mrs McDougall for Rory. Deborah's clad in long black boots and a vulgar leather basque thing and Jeffrey's got on the most revolting black moulded leather pants. She's flicking out her tongue with the dangly ball bearing and he's wearing chains which are all hooked up to his nipples! Turns out this dungeon's the inside of a shop they plan to open. They want to sell all these filthy whips and collars and pants and stuff that 'Whipme', my Jeffrey, makes to order! And Deborah, that is, 'Brittney Pierce', will specialise in body piercing and apparently – this is so disgusting – she's pierced my Jeffrey's you-know-what and he wears a ring on it! It's complete perversion! Naturally the local residents are up in arms! The headline says, 'Fetish fun and furore!' Oh, it's all too much for me!

I went straight to the phone, I said, 'Tell me, Jeffrey, tell me this is a sick joke.'

He said, 'Sorry, Mum, but it's good publicity. We're already doing a great trade online.'

'Trade?' I said. 'Trade, Jeffrey, is about being a plumber or an electrician or, for that matter, a TV repairman like your father was. This whipping and piercing... Jeffrey, I'm stunned. You're perverted.'

'Mum, it's our lifestyle,' he said. 'We like it. People like us aren't harming anyone. We're consenting adults.'

I said, 'Don't go all PC on me, Jeffrey. And as regards consenting, I don't remember being asked if I consented. What was my name doing in amongst all this filth?'

'We couldn't help it, Mum,' he said. 'They asked about our background.'

'Good heavens, Jeffrey, I can't take much more of this,' I told him.

'Sorry, Mum,' he said, 'but you'll have to. We're on the six o'clock flight to London tonight. We're doing *Richard and Judy* tomorrow!'

Pipe Dreams

David Pettigrew

'... there was nothing to break the light of the sun'
Words attributed to Chief Ten Bears in the 1860s;
his memory of the plains before the white men came.

My Squaw, she bellows like the ox. She is calling my name, but her great noise offends my ears so I do not answer. Instead, like the hedgehog, I sit very still and hope that she will not realise where I am. I can see her through the narrow gap of my tipi. She stands some distance away and seems to be looking straight at me. But I know she cannot see me squatting like the toad in the gloom of my refuge. I fear that she will approach, but I call on the eagle spirit inside my chest to will her away. Away, squaw, your great groans thunder through my brain. Away, woman, leave your husband in peace. Unblinking like the lizard, she stares in my direction. Her anger is keen and her face red, but no she cannot see me. She shouts again – 'ALAN, WILL YOU *PLEASE* COME IN FOR YOUR DINNER' – and then she steps back inside the patio door, which rattles like the snake when she slams it shut.

She has left me alone and I am satisfied with the power of the eagle spirit. I know that it is strong within me and I know that I have chosen the right path for my life. I return to my painting. It is tradition for a man to decorate the inside of his tipi, although it is hard to work on polythene walls. Buffalo hide is best for tipi. There are no buffalo in Ayrshire but bin-bags will serve. I reach into the tin that hold my son's felt pens and take out the red one.

I am busy painting the great event of my life: the day the

Great Spirit came down from the sky and communicated to me through the body of Clint, our mini dachshund. This happened during the last moon, a time of great stress. At home, Squaw was discontented. She complained that I was not paying attention to her and our boy and spent too many hours watching videos of Westerns. She did not understand that I did this to escape my troubles. At work a cull of the men was taking place. I was told to decide who should be sacrificed, a task which sank me low. One evening I sat at the dining table, struggling with the ache in my conscience. Like the hunted deer, I was fragile and tired. I had no spirit. Then I heard our dog moving quickly from the kitchen, his claws clicking on the floor. I was aware of him coming to sit at my feet. I thought he wanted his bone.

I looked down. He stared up. There was a glow in his normally sedate eyes and when his jaws opened a booming voice emerged. I knew something was not right.

'Alan,' the dog said.

'Yes,' I answered. It felt like the right thing to do.

'I am Wanka Tanka, the Great Spirit, the Wise One From Above who knows better than all other creatures.'

This sounded true. My dog was small but his eyes beamed like glow-worms. I believed it must be big medicine that could make his jaws work up and down just like a man's.

'I have read about you,' I said.

'You have, but now the time has come to listen. Alan, your life falls to the earth like the wounded crow. You have tried hard, but now you must give it up. You have not known it, but your soul was born on the plains and to the plains you must return.' The dog trotted over to the patio and lifted his paw to the glass. He nodded his head towards the grass of the back garden. 'Return to the old ways, Alan. Return to the prairie where the wind blows free and there is nothing to break the light of the sun.'

These were words which made sense. Inside I had heard them all my life, only I had no courage to listen to their lure. But now that the Great Spirit had come down from the sky and had spoken, I knew I could believe them. The dog looked at me with great eyes, a long stare which passed through to my soul. Then he barked, his body wobbled like the jellyfish, and he peed all over the floor.

Squaw bustled in, shrieking when she saw the large puddle the dog had made. 'For Christ's sake Alan, why didn't you let the dog out?' she roared, shooing the beast out of the way.

Still dazzled by the revelation which had changed my life, I could not answer.

'Why didn't you let the dog out?' she demanded again.

I could give her only silence.

She stood above me with unbelief. 'Look, he's peed everywhere.'

But what did I care? I got up and moved her gently aside. I opened the patio door. I stepped through it and onto the plain. The landscape was vast and animal spirits whispered on the breeze. The sky loomed large. There was nothing to break the light of the sun.

I Like a Man in Uniform

Laura Marney

'Here, wait till I tell you,' whispered the hairdresser.

The customer recognised the tone of voice and settled in her chair, ready for something juicy. Her position was however immediately disturbed by the vigorous pumping up of her seat. With every pump of the hairdresser's foot the customer was jerked a little higher until she could see herself in the mirror above the raised shelf. Clumps of wet hair clung to her slackening jowls and dripped on the frayed towel. As she scrutinised her withered face against the empty salon behind, her view was obscured. With a bullfighter's flick, the statuesque hairdresser whipped the caped overall in the air above the customer's head. The pink nylon parachuted down and was tied in a practised bow behind. A long steel tailcomb began to scrape into sections the customer's thin white hair.

'You know wee Janice that comes in don't you?'

The hairdresser looked into the mirror for confirmation but was met by a blank stare.

'Wee Janice Gilmour, her in First Aid Medicare.'

'First Aid Medicare?'

'You know, the first-aid volunteers.' The hairdresser could see that she was going to have to explain this step by step. Shifting her weight she sighed and forced herself to remember that this was a valued customer. With one hand still working the customer's head she bent her long body and pulled the hairpin trolley towards her.

'You've seen them, they do the first aid at the football. Bandaged Mrs Thompson's leg at the gala day last year. Wear the fancy uniforms.'

'Oh aye,' the customer nodded vigorously in the mirror, 'First Aid Medicare, aye.'

The customer inhaled the warm fusty smell of armpit as the hairdresser lifted a baby blue roller from the trolley and began to wind it tightly around a portion of the customer's hair.

'Well you know wee Janice that's in it.'

'Her with the fancy uniform with all the braid on it?' interrupted the customer. 'I didn't know she was first aid, I thought she was in the Sally Ann or something.'

'Oh no, she's high up in it. She's a Staff Officer.'

'Aye, I know who you mean now, the wee lassie, a bit on the dumpy side but a nice wee face. She's high up in it is she? Good for her.'

The hairdresser was relieved that the customer knew Janice Gilmour, the story was pointless otherwise. The varicose veins that entwined her legs began to throb and itch at this time in the afternoon; telling a racy story would take her mind off her sore legs.

The customer asked, 'Is she not married to the undertaker?'

Confirmation came in a slow nod via the mirror. 'Aye, George Gilmour,' the hairdresser's tone changed to a singsong of sympathy, 'he's an awful nice big man, I mean, I know he's an undertaker and all that but he's a lovely man. I've got a lot of time for George, he's a real gentleman. You'll not meet anyone who doesn't like big George.'

'Aye he did my brother Benny's funeral, an awful nice big man,' crooned the customer.

'Aye well, George's wife,' said the hairdresser returning to the business of the story. 'Janice, she likes the men and she...'

'She does not, does she?' the customer interjected in a scandalised breath, 'she seems that respectable when you see her in her uniform.'

'Oh aye, that's the thing, she loves a man in a uniform, any kind of uniform.'

'Has she not got kids that lassie? I'm sure I've seen her with a couple of kids.'

'Aye she's got kids, but she likes her fun and the more braid on the uniform the better.'

'Well I suppose if you're gonnae do it you might as well do it with an officer,' the customer reasoned. 'Not too tight hen, you know I like the softer wave,' she suggested as her head was being yanked backwards. The hairdresser had a reputation for rough treatment, brushing so forcefully the customer imagined grooves left in her scalp. The customer would have preferred to have her hair done at a proper salon in the city but it was too long a journey and really more than her pension could stretch to. She always asked for a softer wave but always when the hairdresser said, 'Is that alright for you?' she would smile and say, 'That's lovely,' before going home and tousling it into a more relaxed style. She didn't want to look like Maggie Thatcher.

'Oh Janice has had them all: police, firemen, ambulance men, anything with a uniform.'

The customer laughed, 'You sound as if you fancy it yourself, eh, d'you not? A big polis mibbe?'

She had meant this as a bit of fun but the hairdresser reddened and began jacking the seat up even higher. At this height the customer's elastic-stockinged legs dangled in the air.

'She even did it with a bus driver up the back of the bus.'

'She did not!'

The hairdresser was pleased to note that the customer was now shocked.

'No but wait till I tell you.' She had only been setting the scene. The story hadn't even begun yet. 'Can I get you a coffee?'

The hairdresser knew how to spin it out; she wanted the story to last until she had finished dressing the customer's head. If she didn't keep talking her mind would wander back to her varicose veins.

'Aye, thanks, hen.'

The customer was in no rush either; she only came to the hairdressers once a week and every moment of it was to be savoured. Despite the tight curls and the rough handling, she loved the hairdresser's gossip. It seemed the hairdresser only came to life when she was divulging scandal. When she didn't gossip she was sullen and moaned about her veins and her back and how bad business was. The customer often privately wondered why the hairdresser was in this business, with all the bending that was involved. She was too tall for hairdressing, anyone could have told her that.

'Well, the inevitable happened,' said the hairdresser as she handed over a glass cup half filled with coffee. 'She started to see this one guy on a regular basis.'

'Oh aye,' said the customer knowingly, 'and she started to have feelings for him. Did she say whether he had feelings for her?'

'What? Eh, I don't know,' said the hairdresser with gritty irritation.

The customer immediately realised her mistake, she should not have asked, she had broken an unwritten law. The hairdresser was scrupulous about protecting her sources, it was best to stay quiet and let her get on with the tale.

'Anyway, she started to see the guy, Peter, a big fireman, quite a lot. The thing is, she wasn't even doing it with him. This was just after the thing with the bus driver and she was disgusted with herself, I mean, a bus driver, it's not much of a uniform is it? So, she didn't even do it for about two months and then when she did, it wasn't even any good.'

'Why did she keep on seeing him then if it wasn't any good?' the customer couldn't help asking.

'I don't know, maybe she was just lonely.'

'And it wasn't any good?'

'Och you know the kind of thing, he, Peter, couldn't control himself.'

The hairdresser lowered her voice to a hiss, pronouncing her words more precisely while screwing up her face and pointing downwards, 'Down there, too quick.'

The customer never ceased to be amazed at the detail the hairdresser would come up with. Who would have told her such intimate details? It had to be Janice Gilmour herself, either that or the hairdresser was making it up, colouring in the detail from her own imagination.

The hairdresser had completed a neat track of baby blue rollers that ran from the brow to the nape of the customer's neck, giving the appearance of a mohican. She now groped for the larger orange rollers from the trolley as she continued with the story.

'He knew the score, knew she was married, but he was getting serious, kept giving her wee gifts and that. Peter wasn't much fun though. Too heavy. It's understandable. He'd only recently split up with his wife, he was probably still upset about that. Plus, his mother wasn't keeping well and he was running up and down to the hospital visiting her all the time.'

The hairdresser paused for a moment to replenish the stock of hairpins that she held in the corner of her mouth. 'Did you see George on *Scotland Today*?'

The customer was startled by the question.

'Sorry?'

The hairdresser took the pins out of her mouth and used the voice she kept for her deaf customers or those under the drier. '*I'M SAYING, DID YOU SEE GEORGE ON* SCOTLAND TODAY?'

'*NO I DIDN'T SEE IT, WAS GEORGE ON IT*?' said the customer just as slow and loud. Just because we're old she thinks we're daft, thought the customer. I was a Sales Department Assistant Manageress. Just because I'm sixty-six doesn't mean I couldn't buy and sell her, she thought. The customer set her face in a defiant huff.

The hairdresser caught the reprimand and was momentarily flustered. She couldn't afford to fall out with customers. She must remember that her OAP trade sustained the business. Must not dwell on the impulse to scream at them or drive hairpins into their thin skulls. She needed their custom, unlike them, she had no comfortable pension.

'Yeah, big George was on it last Thursday night, he saved a wee girl's life at the ice rink. He gave first aid and they interviewed him on *Scotland Today*.' The hairdresser had managed to coax a friendly tone from her throat.

'Oh aye! Brenda was telling me about that! That wee girl's heart stopped you know, Brenda knows her mother.' In her excitement the customer forgot her huff. Through her brother Benny's funeral and knowing someone who knew the wee girl's mother, she had a connection to one of the main players and now felt personally involved in the story. 'God, imagine that. Big George was it? I didn't know he did the first aid as well.'

'Aye, he's a volunteer first aider.'

'He's an undertaker *and* a first aider?'

'Aye. So either he saves their lives or he buries his mistakes.' The hairdresser tried out a conciliatory smile.

'Well, I suppose either way, he gets the business!' squawked the customer, delighted with her own witty riposte.

'Aye, that's a good one!' the hairdresser chuckled, relieved to be on good terms again. She was keen to return to the story before the customer remembered her huff. 'Peter was on the backshift and he saw George Gilmour on the telly. I mean, he's not daft is he? He must have realised when he heard the name George Gilmour giving first aid that it was Janice's husband.'

'He knew it was her man!' exclaimed the customer, catching on.

'He knew fine well.'

The customer's head was finished and the heavily perfumed smell of setting lotion now filled the air as the hairdresser began dousing the rollers with a wad of cotton wool.

'Well,' she continued, getting in to her stride, 'that's when it started: leave your husband, leave George and come and live with me, he says.'

The customer had her eyes screwed shut tight against the nippy drips of the setting lotion.

'She didn't go, did she? She's never left her kids and that good man of hers, has she?'

'Not on your Nelly,' said the hairdresser, fiercely jabbing each roller in turn, 'Janice had to tell him it was over. He took it bad, plus, at the same time, his mother died.'

'Oh, God, what of?' The customer could only make short replies. She hated this bit, her head was pushed all the way back against the hairdresser's brown gingham nylon overall.

'I don't know, the usual I think, cancer.'

'Terrible.'

'Och he was probably just saying it but he started making threats about how he was going to tell her man.'

'Oh for goodness sake.'

Layered on top of the strong chemical smell of the setting lotion, with their faces inches apart, the customer could now smell cheese and onion crisps from the hairdresser's breath.

'Said he was going to tell George everything, then she would have to come and live with him because if George was any kind of a man he would put her out of the house, says Peter.'

With one last powerful dab the customer was released from the headlock. She stretched her neck forward a bit to get the feeling back. 'See? That's what happens, you play with fire you get burned. She should've stuck to flings.'

'Uh hu,' agreed the hairdresser, tidying away the lotion.

'Well? Did he? Did he tell George?'

The hairdresser hunched her large frame forward, 'Well it was a bit of a turn up for the books because...'

The chime on the door rang and alerted them that they were no longer alone in the shop. The hairdresser immediately moved towards the reception desk and spoke quietly to the young man who had just come in.

'I'm busy just now and I've got a four o'clock coming in, can you come back at half four?'

The customer didn't realise she had been holding her breath

until she exhaled heavily as the chimes rang again when the young man left the shop.

She almost shouted, 'So did he tell George?'

'It was at his mother's funeral,' the hairdresser continued smoothly as she stretched a brown hair net over the crash helmet of rollers, 'Peter had left all the arrangements to his sister.'

'Typical man.'

'So there he was, sitting in the church large as life when who should walk in but big George.'

The customer sucked in her breath loudly, 'George was the undertaker for Peter's mother!'

'Yep, and what does George do but walk straight up to Peter and sit beside him in the pew.'

'George went up and sat beside him? Oh my God, in front of all his family? And at a time like that. So what did George say to him?'

'Nothing.'

'Nothing?'

'Well he said he was sorry that his mother had died and he spoke about the arrangements for carrying the coffin and all that but he didn't *say* anything.'

'What did Peter do, then? I thought he was threatening to tell George everything? Did he tell him?'

This was the hairdresser's favourite bit, the big finish: 'His mother's lying there in the coffin, his whole family around him and Peter starts saying how he was really sorry and that he hadn't meant for it to happen.'

'Oh my God! What did George say?'

'Well that's the thing.' The hairdresser leaned forward and

brought her head level. Compelling the customer's full attention in the mirror, her eyes grew large and her words heavy with significance. 'George just looks him square in the eye and says, you're upset just now son, with your mother dying and everything, you'll feel a lot better when you put all this behind you.'

'When you put all this behind you? What did he mean by that? Did he know?' Again the door chime rang.

This time a woman entered, a small dumpy woman with a pretty face wearing a first-aid officer's uniform.

'Janice, you're early, I wasn't expecting you until four,' said the hairdresser, a little flummoxed.

'Och, is that all the time is? I didn't realise I was early, d'you want me to come back?'

'Eh, well...' the hairdresser thought for a moment. 'Och no you're fine, I was just going to stick this lady under the drier.'

As she was being wheeled across the salon in her elevated chair the customer called out, 'Hello Mrs Gilmour, how are you? How's that nice husband of yours? He's a lovely big man, he did my brother Benny's funeral so he did. Still at the undertaking is he?'

The hairdresser wasted no time in lifting the hood on the drier and clamping the customer inside. She switched the fan on full power so that the customer did not hear Janice Gilmour's affable reply. Under the heat and noise of the drier the customer could see the two women laughing and chatting away like old friends as the hairdresser began combing Janice Gilmour's hair into sections.

Creatures from the Blue Lagoon

Jas Sherry

Monday: Pete
Kandinsky

I was at the window when the van drew up. Printed along its side in bright blue lettering – Blue Lagoon Co. – Kitchen & Bathroom Specialists – a silhouette of a mermaid perched on the ampersand. A man clambered from the cabin, dressed in navy-blue overalls. Over his shoulder, a dark-blue bag – the tools of his trade. As he strolled across the road he glanced up and caught me retreating from the window. The door-entry system buzzed.

He was youngish, early twenties. His first words were, 'Sorry for being this late.' With something akin to x-ray vision he scanned my face, breasts, hips, thighs. I led him to the bathroom. He dropped his bag and removed a slice of paper from his pouch. He turned it one way, then another, held it up to light, tilted his head, smiled. 'I think I've got it,' he said. He donned his tool belt and told me he needed to get a few things from the van.

When he returned I said, 'Listen, I have to make an interview in about half-an-hour, can I leave you to get on with things? My partner will pop in soon. You can discuss the specifics then.'

'Nice perfume,' he remarked, as I hurried to go. 'Thanks,' I replied, inside a faked smile.

'I'll have to turn your water off,' he revealed. I led him to the kitchen and pointed down towards where I thought the stopcock might be. 'Very nice,' he quipped, his finger aimed at the Kandinsky. 'What's it meant to be, exactly?' 'An abstract, I suppose.' 'An abstract what?' 'An abstract anything really. A colourful pattern, pleasing to the eye'. 'Goes well with the rest of the place,' the young man decided. 'That's why we like it,' I said. 'By the way, my name's Pete,' he said, with a twinkle. His right hand extended towards me. 'I'm Susan,' I said, placing mine inside his.

As he held my hand, his eyes grazed the slopes of my cleavage.

Tuesday: Chic
Commando

The tile snapped cleanly as he warmed to his subject. 'Everyone loves us,' he proclaimed, 'everywhere we go they love the Scots – France, Greece, Scandinavia, Russia, all over the shop. Except for the Irish perhaps, too close in temperament, Celtic blood and all that. The English obviously. They hate us, we hate them. Everyone hates them with their Jimmy Hill certificates in arrogance, the never-ending story of Wembley sixty-six. A fix if ever there was one.' He squeezed another tile neatly into place. 'But the Scots? Nae bother. Tell ye why. Foreigners. They all love the kilt they do, crazy for it. Many a time when we were on tour wi the Tartan Army we hardly had to spend a thing. Soon as they clocked the old kilt it wis free drink all round and no kidding. There wis always that wee bit of mystery, y'know – is he or isn't he? Is he, or is he no, a real Scotsman? How we swirled and twirled and birled many a night away. Drove them mad we did.' He snapped another.

'One time these wee French lassies come over. They start pointing and what have ye, expressing things in French that needed no translation. So a whole squad of us got intae line and then it was 1-2-3, *viva la difference*. Magic.' He pressed a tile hard into the wall and mopped his brow. He fell to silence. The spreading of the word. Tales of Scottish camaraderie and *joie de vivre*.

When he finished off he asked me to come and pass verdict on his labour. He had managed to tile most of the small area in under two hours, fuelled by thoughts of good times gone and good times to come, his frame lubricated with giant intakes of Irn Bru. He wiped over the tiles with a rag to give them a shine. As he bent down, I noticed how the broad elastic of his underpants crept high above the waist of his trousers, hugging the small of his back.

Fah, a long, long way to run.

Wednesday: Sammy
A Saucerful of KitKats

After some hours huffing and puffing he slouched through to the kitchen where I was seated, pouring over the job section of *The Herald*. 'Any chance a cuppa?' he asked. 'Sure,' I said, 'take a pew. What do you prefer, tea, coffee?' 'Tea please, two sugar, and a splash of milk,' he answered. As the kettle began to heat, I prepared a mug and a saucerful of KitKats.

'Oh good,' he said, 'KitKats, my favourite.' 'It's all we've got,' I replied, 'how are things going, anyway?' 'Hard work,' he sighed, 'having some trouble. Trouble getting the eh y'know the eh unit to fit into the eh, y'know. Don't worry,' he said, with an unconvincing tone. The kettle clicked. I poured out the coffee and placed it beside the small pile of biscuits. He tore open one wrapper and munched the chocolate fingers with relish. 'I like KitKats,' he said. I returned to the job section. 'Looking for a job then, what you do exactly?' 'I'm er a nurse', I said, untruthfully, expecting my nose to extend several metres.

'I been in hospitals a few times. Have lots of respect for nurses I have. Can't be easy.' He shook his head and his mane of hair flopped from side to side. 'When I was in with my big toe there was this lovely wee thing. Nurse Kelly with lovely red hair. I fell in love with those flowing locks I did. Still have dreams sometimes. Or was it the time I had trouble downstairs? Bit foggy these days.' He devoured his second Kitkat with force and reached out for his hat trick. 'These are lovely,' he insisted, oblivious to my stocktaking. 'The wife, she doesn't have KitKats, gets the cheaper brand from the supermarket whatever. Not the same,' he winced. 'Toothache;

shouldn't be having these really.' 'I prefer Twix Bars myself,' I said. 'Yeah? So do I,' he said, nodding his mane and munching. 'Love Twixes I do, but KitKats take the biscuit.' He began a giggle that quickly turned to violent fits of coughing. Victim of his own wordplay.

Thursday: Eric
Kindertotenlieder

While he worked he chirped like a bird. I could hear him twitter above the radio which was set at low volume, dial lodged at Radio 3. Less distracting than other stations. Chores become less like chores if a soundtrack is provided. Like the movies and the chirping of birds. Can ironing ever be made enjoyable? That's what I was doing while the chirpy fellow hammered intermittently during the season of Mahler. A day of songs announced the voice.

He had arrived with a smile and went straight to work – an orchestra of hammers and drills. His melodic doodles brought an alien counterpoint to his chance composition. I was struggling with the sleeves of a shirt when his head popped in. Little beads of sweat speckled his forehead.

His lunch came wrapped in tinfoil. Banana sandwiches. I poured hot water into his personalised mug. 'Best Dad in the World' it read. An aromatic smell bled from a tea bag.

He stirred the spoon and chirped some more. The radio became preoccupied with the unfolding of that day's news. The BBC voice droned on in the background as the world's best dad tucked into sandwiches and sipped tea politely. The beads of sweat had evaporated and his skull took on a metallic sheen. We spoke of the weather. Too hot, too cold, too in-between. His thin moustache glistened with herb tea and banana. He produced a carton of yoghurt from his satchel, a plastic spoon from his sleeve. A voice returned us to the studio.

When the music reappeared it sounded sad. The best dad

turned pale. He kept his eyes fixed upon the debris of his lunch. He scrunched the tinfoil and began to cry. I didn't realise it at first until a tear dropped. 'Can I help?' I asked. All he said was, the music.

Within minutes he was back at work crashing and banging with hammer and drill, chirping all the while. Sometimes life comes with its own soundtrack.

Friday: Mr Noon

Our Motto

Mr Noon arrived at nine sharp. He brought an air of efficiency and a clipboard nestled in his left arm. He wiped the soles of both shoes in a precise even rhythm. His head entered followed by torso followed by two clean shoes. Very nice, he remarked, very nice indeed. His head moved up and down in slow oscillations. 'Lived here long?' he enquired. 'About, um, seven years,' I admitted, after some shaky arithmetic. I ushered him to the bathroom and apologised for the clothing scattered over the radiator. 'Quite alright,' he said, 'I've seen everything there is to see.'

A methodical man was Mr Noon. His head swivelled from angle to angle, taking in the whole interior. He began submitting details to his clipboard. I asked him if he fancied a cup of coffee since I was about to have one. 'Not for me,' he insisted, 'a quick run down the checklist and I'll be on my way.' I left him to it and slipped through to the kitchen. I switched off the radio, poured out my coffee, grabbed the last KitKat and returned to find him staring into the mirror above the sink. He swivelled and grinned through a small gap in his front teeth.

'So,' he began, 'you are quite satisfied with the way all works have been carried out?' I told him about the door not opening smoothly, the hairline crack in the shower tray, how certain tiles did not seem to match and the fact that the shower control sat askew. He directed his eyes to the clipboard, then to the shower, then to me, then to the clipboard, then back to me. He released a long descending sigh and slumped to the rim of the bath. He began to scribble across the clipboard in red biro. His face grew crimson in proportion to the amount of scribble.

'I will have to advise the manager about these matters,' he declared. 'Blue Lagoon promise perfection. Perfection, after all, is our motto.' 'That's quite reassuring,' I said. 'In the interim...' he began, but, for some reason, he let a long pause linger in the air. A pause into which bird song soon flitted, in and out. 'Can I, perhaps, use your bathroom? For the purpose of convenience I mean.' He rushed in and the soft click of the snib told me the door had fastened tight.

After an interval of some twenty minutes, I approached the locked door and hailed, 'Are you alright?' No reply came. I became concerned and called again. I thought I detected a faint grunt. I waited. Finally the snib slid back. Mr Noon appeared looking rather pale. He sat for some time and managed to drain a glass of cool tap water. He left soon after with all manner of apologies ringing the air. Later, I was disturbed to notice the curious rearrangement of certain items of underwear.

Brochan

Martin MacIntyre

A weekday morning, call it Wednesday and we are talking and negotiating about porridge. Our word for this gluey Scottish staple is brochan. I presume that the substance of our magical ordinary discussion may well be being replicated in other Edinburgh homes. The music however has to be different. Bleary-eyed bedrobed dads stirring hopefully; eager two-and-a-half year olds flitting between instilled starvation and the wonders of each ever-clearer new morning. While I generally prepare Sorcha's brochan, it was always my mother who placed porridge before the three of us. Her flimsy nylon dressinggown swished dangerously close to two quite ratty old electric bars.

Apparently my father knew how to make real porridge, just like his grandmother used to: coarse oats steeped overnight in loch water, the secret mixture bubbled slowly on a peat stove, warm frothy cow's milk crowning the top. Brochan would have been their generic term also but at a guess they may have had another twenty words to describe the preparatory steps, phases and byproducts of this simple cuisine. Brochan for them really was a staple. Its absence could mean starvation. Alas, or perhaps fortunately, I never had occasion to taste this exotic dish, but was thrilled to find and buy two packets of medium grain oatmeal in Sainsbury's on Sunday.

Sorcha is beautiful. In the morning she is exquisite. Her trusting cuddles induce a rush of emotions which, if they demanded instant definition, would certainly lead to a small pot encrusted with inedible, sad, black brochan. I am happy to tell her I love her and to return to erratic plopping. Turn down the heat and await consistency. Never the same two days running, never the same feelings, never the same amount in her or my bowl, never any salt or sugar added.

I ask her about her dreams, half rhetorically. She smiles and gives a list of older cousins who occupy a small frame on top of her shared chest of drawers. Her evolving boundaries are open at the ends allowing day and night, past and present, Mammy, Daddy to share her world fluidly. She has much to learn and teach. She loves her cousins. Last time they met, at the Mod in Dunoon, she greeted them all with a huge kiss and cuddle. She has effortlessly picked up the first verse of the song that Michelle, the oldest of the three, performed. She heard her sing it a couple of times. My daughter's innocent voice sings so sweetly of eighteenth-century forced emigration from Kintail and in the same undifferentiated breath, of the generosity of *Baa Baa Black Sheep*. She often breaks into song between spoonfuls. Not today. Should I tune in to Radio 4? No, not today.

'*Tuilleadh Bainne* (More milk)!' A gleeful giggle, what will Daddy do this morning?

It's an old routine but still quite amusing. She asks for more milk in her green plastic cup, ostensibly to drink, but then if I don't make a fuss she pours it all on top of the porridge without drinking any of it. If I do remonstrate, she tries to bargain that she will drink most of it and only pour a small amount on the porridge. Depending on how much milk she has drunk, how much is left floating un-supped on top of her porridge and how strong a disciplinarian I am that particular morning – a decision is reached. Never the same two days running, perhaps showing flexibility, perhaps lacking consistency.

Today she has worked her way through a hearty bowl that would lighten the day for many a teenager's tense parents. There are around three spoonfuls remaining to allow Winnie the Poo to be fully revealed.

She refuses help.

'*Tha mi buidheach* (I am quite full).'

Sorcha has evidently eaten enough porridge today and she expresses her repleteness casually but firmly. She chooses words that are so ordinary in villages contained within a ten-mile radius of her great-grandmother's ruined dwelling and upturned cooking vessels in South Uist. So ordinary that local children there may not realise that they have gone. So extraordinary in Edinburgh that Radio 4 seems much more familiar and safe.

A Drop in the Ocean

Jim Trevorrow

'Is it yourself Sandy? Man, but it must be near five years since you were last here.' The scent of the firs that clung to the hillside, mingled with that of fresh cut timbers scattered about the yard. Hyacinth spread a blue carpet over the bright green bracken, with its pockets of bright primroses.

'Seven to be precise.' The other's bulk filled the doorway of the carpenter's shop, casting an oblique shadow against the morning sun.

'Come away ben; I heard you were in the village. See what I caught for you.'

'It's true then Calum, you *were* out last night with the nets?'

'Aye…' The boatbuilder's face creased in a grin; a little leprechaun of a man, sharp chinned, with wild wispy grey hair, sticking out from under his bunnet.

'The salmon was running, so I went out in the dark with the boat. I've had a fair catch. I'll show you!' He led the way through the shop and yard into the stone cottage. On the kitchen table were five large salmon laid side by side. 'What do ye say tae that?'

'Oh aye,' his companion rejoined, 'that's a fine catch for the dark.' He knew that Calum would have stretched out his nets from the shore long before that night, waiting on the salmon returning to their spawning grounds. 'Morag will be here, will she, to gut the fish?'

'It's odd right enough, I would have thought she would have been about by now, but there's no sign of the lass this morning.' The lass was well over seventy years old, and Calum's wife. 'Maybe she has popped down to the shop? She'll likely be havin a blether wi' Maisie MacDonald.'

'She wasn't in the post office when I passed it.' Sandy made that observation before sitting himself down on a sturdy wooden chair, next to the table. He'd arrived at Glen Arlich on the previous evening's steamer and spent the night at the Ailsa Hotel. 'I watched you bring *The Meg Merrilees* in this morning: what age is she now?'

Calum took off his bunnet and scratched his thatch, 'She'll be... Och the same age as my old mither would have been if she had survived... That would make her about ninety-eight years old. Mind you, the way she sails she is as sprightly as ever she was.'

'You keep her in fine trim then?'

'Aye. A good boat is a good friend, and times I take the mail out in her. I use the petrol engine now and again but only if the wind drops.' *The Meg Merrilees* was a large sailing smack, capable of carrying coals if it came to the bit. Though by then, most freight came by steamer from Gourock, or puffer from Glasgow.

Sandy stretched out his long legs under the table. 'You're still managing then to keep the business running?'

'As you say! Folk are aye deein or wantin their boats repaired although there is more in the first category these days than in the second.' Coughing, he rose from his chair and went to the back door to spit. 'Times is not what they used to be. Young folk are all off to the city for jobs and the like. Trade is fallin off; so it is. Mind you there is no the same call with the yaats as there used to be. I put it doon tae the Labour government, fair knocked the bottom oot the merkat, an awfu shame, what wi that and Bakelite and this newfangled fibre glass. For centuries we've made do wi wood, and comes the War; in its wake the Yankees have given us straw glass tae mend oor boats wi. As weel they're no usin them fur coffins yet, or a wad be oot o work awthegither.' He lowered himself back into the chair opposite, 'Man but we've missed you over the years. There's a few has come gone in your place but never a one to match you. They don't make the polis the wey they used too, neither they do. Morag herself says they broke the mould and threw it away, after you wis born. So what brings you back to your old haunts?'

'Old friends, Calum, old times' sake and gossip.'

'Is that so?' The leprechaun clasped his long thin hands together. 'I might have guessed that it wasnae just a pleasure trip.'

From the window of the cottage Sandy had a broad view of the loch, with the abutting carpenter's shop, boatyard sheds and slipways running down to the water's edge. As placid and peaceful a scene as anyone could want to see, the high purpling green of Ben Arlich, towering its rocky crown against a pastel blue sky. He shook his head solemnly and said, 'There is a lot of talk about Morag. Some as say she has not been seen this last week and before that she was lookin gey ill.'

'Havers, Sandy nothin but havers. You ask Maisie MacDonald and she'll put you straight. Morag was as right as rain yesterday, you can see how she's made up the fire ready for kindling.' With a long thin arm, the old man pointed to the fireplace on his left. The grate was empty of anything but a few cinders and ash left over from its last lighting.

Sandy spoke as though he had noticed nothing, 'Jock Mclean was worried. Some story you told him about Morag going down to Dunoon to visit her sister.' The anxious look left the carpenter's face, a big smile, making it almost cherubic.

'Of course, of course,' he exclaimed with the eagerness of a child, 'that's right. It's to see Susan, how could I forget.' There was a sense of relief in his voice. 'She must have told Dr Mclean she was going.' Then he stopped with some confusion. 'But she was here last night, I am sure she was here last night, I was speaking to her myself.' He nodded sagely to his friend. 'She must have caught the early morning steamer.' A conspiratorial gleam came into his eyes. Afraid of being overheard, he leaned across the table and spoke in a low voice, 'Tis all because of them, Sandy. They come and they go as they please, walkin aboot the hoose.' His lower lip stuck out and his stubbled chin wagged.'

'Oh aye,' Sandy's replied, 'have you any notion who they might be?' With a frightened look on his face the old man shook his head, 'Time was, they wadnae go ony farther than the embalming room; then they was comin into the boathoose and the carpenters' shop. I telt them tae go away, but it made nae difference at aw; in fact they got worse, the very devil they were.' He sighed, 'It must hae been too much for her and she decided tae go aff tae see Susan. She should have telt me though she was goin on the *Ivanhoe*.'

'Too much for her?' Sandy asked. Like Dr Mclean he knew that Susan Cameron, Morag's older sister had been dead some fifteen years. The *Ivanhoe* had been scrapped thirty years before and the early morning sailing from Glen Arlich pier discontinued when the railway steamers were first nationalised,

'She wouldnae take my word that they were there you sees, a' we had a fair old argument, "Seein is believin' " I telt her. But she would have none of it. "Silly old eediot," she ca'd me.' He sighed, 'Man and boy, the first argument I ever had wi her in sixty years. She said, she wished she could be with her sister Susan, she was aye closest tae her.'

The old man looked up at Sandy apprehensively, 'Wheest man... they're here again!' He looked furtively over his shoulder, and said in a low voice, 'Pay no attention to them, they'll no touch you, they never as much as have a word tae say onyways.' The policeman looked at his old friend; the house was silent and there was no sign of anyone at all. Calum gave him a meaningful glance. 'They just walk through; nae harm in it I suppose.'

Sandy's curiosity was roused. 'Are there any kent faces among them Calum, that you remember?' The patriarchal boatbuilder just shook his head and said no more, staring silently at the floor. After a silence that seemed to drag forever, Calum raised his head again,

'Aye!' He said in satisfaction, 'that's them done: like I told you they would, they have gone away.' Sandy, considerably worried, tried a change of tack, 'I wonder if they've done any damage in the other rooms? Maybe we should go and have a look?'

'Just the very thing to do!' Calum leapt to his feet. 'There's mischief in them for sure.'

In his easy, relaxed way, Sandy said casually, 'I'll have a look in the wardrobe.'

They were in the master bedroom. The double bed was there; its sheets hardly disturbed; by appearance it looked unlikely that anyone had slept there overnight. Morag's silver hairbrush, comb and vanity mirror were in prominence on the old fashioned oak dressing table beside her ointment jars and a large earthenware jug filled with clear water. He opened the wardrobe door; a number of dresses were hanging inside and Morag's coats, but no other sign of the woman herself.

'I seen them in the spare bedrooms, so I did,' Calum said, voice angry with affronted dignity, 'they are kept for the family, no for the likes of them strangers.' In the first and largest, faded photographs of the boys were hanging on the walls, both had died long ago in the Battle of the Somme. A large badly painted portrait of Marjorie, their daughter, hung over the mantelpiece in the small room. Sadly, she had been knocked down and killed by a bus in Glasgow, during a blackout in the Second World War. Morag's forlorn mementoes of her sons were still there on top of the empty beds: young Calum's fishing line, Murdo's tin whistle. The china-faced doll wearing the Darvel lace dress and bonnet, sat propped up on the mantelpiece of the girl's room. He could spot no other evidence of occupancy. Relief showed on the old man's face, 'Aye you were aye a good influence in the hoose,' he said with a satisfied smile. 'They have takin the measure of yourself and cleared off; not a trace to be seen of them anyhow.' To reassure themselves they had a look in the privy, spotlessly clean as Morag always kept it.

The police officer could see no indication of the old lady's presence. None of the fires were lit and there was a sad damp feel about the house. During his years as a raw bachelor village constable, before he had been promoted to the CID, Sandy had spent many warm and happy evenings at their fireside.

Whoever Calum's mysterious visitors were, they had proved invisible to the eyes of the law. 'Tis them,' the old man says, 'as might be in the timber shed or the saw mill.' With a smile, Sandy suggested, 'We'll try there then; we'll have a look to make sure.' In all seriousness Calum's eyes were bright blue and his gaze fixed on the big police officer, 'The likes of you, it is that we've been needin here all this last while.'

He led the way through the garden back into the boatyard muttering as he went, 'A proper polisman, that's to keep them at bay.'

'Aye don't worry, Calum, if I catch sight of your visitors, they'll soon get their marching orders. Let's make a thorough search.' Fortunately Calum caught no further glimpses of them.

Everything was in good order in the yard, only one small boat pulled up on the slipway, Sandy lifted the canvas cover and inspected its interior. It was empty. Moored at the long timber jetty, *The Meg Merrilees* sails were snugly lowered and tied down, her hold empty, the fishing nets coiled abaft in the cockpit. The carpenter's shop, timber yard, saw room, net store and sail loft, were as the old man proudly said, 'All shipshape and in Bristol fashion.' There was no sign of any activity other than that of the boat builder's neat and tidy mind. Least of all was there any sign of Morag, alive or dead. Sandy had taken every opportunity to look in cupboards, under tables, in odd corners. He had open and shut doors, even the lids of boxes. His host delighted at having his story apparently treated with some seriousness, sounding an accolade of praise at his friend's diligence. Eventually they came to a primitive lean-to shed which served as mortuary and embalming room. Calum threw the door open to flood it with the morning sunshine. There, lying flat on the middle of the workbench was a new beech wood coffin, surrounded by fawn and red wood shavings. The scent of fresh polish was strong. The lid unusually was held on one side with brass hinges which gleamed in the sun. An unengraved brass plate had been screwed to its face.

'You have a funeral then?' Sandy asked. 'Who has died?'

Calum glowered. 'Naebody died: I just made the coffin to keep my hand in; trade has been slack this while. You see, a lovely finish as good as ever I've done; lead lined and padded inside too. None of your Bakelite rubbish or pine wood and veneer.' He was rightly proud of the craftsmanship displayed. Sandy walked over to make a closer examination. The coffin was empty.

'An act of faith,' Calum said. 'There is a man lives on the other side of the loch, an Englishman, who saw it and has taken a notion to buy it.'

'He will be a little man then?' Sandy asked, casting a critical eye at the coffin.

'Aye, aboot the same size as myself.'

The police officer realised too that it would as easily fit Morag. There was nothing else for it but to nod. Even if he came back with a warrant and a squad to take the place apart, they would stand little chance of discovering if Morag was dead, or if her spouse had buried her. When Calum's back was turned, he gathered a sample of the shavings, and popped them into his jacket pocket, though he wasn't sure why. He would go back to Jock Mclean and report his findings. Steps would have to be taken for Calum to be 'looked after.' A pity that it had come to that; it was plain to see that the man was deluded. God help me, Sandy thought, if ever I get to be like that.

The doctor and he spent the evening discussing what could be done. Telephone calls were made. A specialist would come from the city to see Calum for himself. Meanwhile they would keep an eye on the old man between them and the local constable. 'It's over a week since anyone in the village saw Morag,' Mclean said. 'She didn't leave on the steamer, as you know yourself.' No one had seen her on the road over Devil's Pass, which in any case was no place for an old woman on foot. Little better than two thin strips of tarmac with grass growing between, it provided the only alternative route from the village. Dr Mclean continued, 'I was pleased you were able to come. We've been at our wit's end here, and now you have been promoted to Detective Inspector, I was sure you could put the wheels in motion. Calum would never have let anyone else into his secret in any case.'

Long shadows were cast by the evening sun as it fell below Ben Arlich. Sandy and the physician, sat on the porch of the Doctor's house enjoying the view of the loch. '*The Meg Merrilees*!' The inspector exclaimed suddenly, as he saw the old sailing smack launch out from Calum's Boatyard farther along the shore, and set course for the opposite coast. He lifted the doctor's field glasses and focused on the craft, 'Of course I should have thought of that. We'll have to borrow a motor boat from the pier and get after him. He has the coffin aboard: maybe we could stop him before he dumps it in the sea.' Even as they climbed into the doctor's car and drove down to the pier he was uneasy, something he knew or had seen and overlooked irked him.

When they caught up with *The Meg* she was sailing with the offshore breeze behind her; mainsail set, tiller lashed, and crewless. The scratch marks on her gunwale where the coffin had gone over the side were quite clear. The trestles that had supported the coffin on the deck were still in place. The two men were dumbfounded,

'He's dropped her in the sea!' Mclean said.

'No, I don't think so, not tonight anyhow.' Sandy was still grappling with the sailing smack's tiller, when he turned to the doctor. 'That coffin fixing was quite different from the usual; it was hinged on one side and there were no screws.' He stopped speaking as he realised the implications of his words. 'There were bolts on the underside of the lid. I didn't think about it at the time, but my guess is they were designed to be slipped into place from inside. I think Calum has buried himself at sea!' After a pause he added, 'I should have realised there were too many shavings for one coffin.' Judging by the colour of the wood shavings the first coffin had been made of mahogany, more than likely lead lined too, and probably dropped overboard on the night when he arrived. I don't suppose we will ever know if he killed her, or if she died of natural causes and he only buried her.'

The waters of Loch Arlich were deemed to be as deep as the mountains on either side were high. Sandy was sure that his two friends lay in the fathoms below the looming shape of Ben Arlich, together now in death as they had been in life.

Never Lived

Kathy Daly

When you die, I shall go to Paris. I will carry you with me as we visit all the places I dreamed of, that you told me about. Then I'll say goodbye, before I scatter you from the top of the Eiffel Tower.

At fifteen I developed a penchant for Frenchmen's noses. While my friends huddled over their mothers' magazines, bonding over their adoration of Tom Cruise and Patrick Swayze, I was alone with my black and white photos of Gerard Dépardieu and Alain Delon, ripped out of a magazine in the doctor's surgery.

It began the first time I saw Bernard Bonnaire. He was standing at the PE department, smoking a small brown cigar. There was nothing covert about his habit, nor the usual desperate sucking I hated so much. He was straight out of one of those classic monochrome photos – shoulder length hair, sallow face and a large nose. Everything else was compact and in proportion – apart from his nose. It was even more breathtaking in profile. It was beautiful.

Monsieur Bernard, as he asked us to call him, was our substitute French teacher. Suddenly I progressed from an average French student to the top of my class. I had to know everything about France: its culture; its language. I read guide books, literature, anything that could impress Bernard. He would intersperse the lesson with stories of his years in Paris. His languid reserve would change to enthusiasm, animation. He infected me with his love for hot chocolate in a quiet café, his soft voice incanting the various place names. It seemed more and more that despite being in a busy classroom, the interchange between us was more deep and meaningful than anyone else could realise.

One Friday afternoon, on a hot clammy May day, we all sat in the French class, waiting for Bernard to come and teach us. I was sitting, flicking through my French book, the words a blur and my stomach gripped with the anticipation of seeing Bernard after a long day of maths, geography and science. He walked into the room, dispensing a smile just for me, 'Bonjour, class.' The heat in the room, the friction of twenty-eight bodies interred there, assailed Bernard. He walked back to the door – 'Everyone, bring your books and pens. Line up. We're going outdoors.'

We followed him out and down through the school. He was carrying a cardboard box with him, which, once outside, he laid down. I sat down on the yellow sun-bleached grass and wondered what was in that box. Bernard began to teach the lesson, but I found it hard to concentrate on what he said. The girls next to me were too busy watching the fifth year boys playing football on the pitch nearby. Bernard gave up. 'It is too hot today. However, I have some refreshments for us.' He opened the crate and handed out bottles of Orangina, then croissants and jam. I bit into the sweet buttery pastry. Bernard gave me a smile and I almost couldn't swallow.

While we were all eating and drinking he told us that the final list of people picked for the Paris trip had been decided, but that we'd have to wait until we returned to class. Bernard voiced regret at not having his guitar.

The rain started, sieved from the bruised sky above. The other girls shrieked and ran towards the school. They were spurred on faster by the thunder, and the boys strode after them. I helped Bernard to retrieve the scattered jotters and put the empty bottles in the box. The rain saturated my school shirt, and Bernard tutted, took off his black sweater and wrapped it round my shoulders.

I felt his hand brush against my shoulders as lightning ripped metallic across the sky. It seemed to strike me, but it was Bernard propelling me through the side entrance of the school. I wanted him to pull me into the corner and kiss me, but instead he and I carried the box back up to class.

While I huddled next to a warm radiator, Bernard was giving out the letters to the people who'd been picked for Paris. He handed one to me. The bell rang and the class emptied. The letter was safely sandwiched between two textbooks, but on the bus home, I still checked four times, just to make sure.

At the supermarket the bus sat for what seemed an eternity. I pulled the cuffs of the black lambswool sweater and scrunched them into my palms, then reran the whole afternoon again in my head. The taste of the croissant, the light sweat behind my neck as I'd sat on the grass, Bernard's hands touching my shoulder, his hand on my wrist as he'd pulled me inside. Soon we'd be in Paris together.

Eventually the bus pulled back into traffic and as we trundled up the hill, a banana-coloured VW beetle turned into a gravel drive in front of a grey Victorian house. The driver got out and I recognised the sweep of the hand through black hair, and the large nose. Bernard walked into the house.

As we drove down the other side of the hill, I added this little scene to the one unfolded earlier. I looked out of the window. The storm hadn't just thrust Bernard and me together, it had also dispelled the humidity, the sweltering misty heat that had blighted us for days and the cool rain had slaked the thirst of the dry grass and trees. Every blade, every leaf was rejuvenated.

When I got off the bus at the busy street near my house, I walked into the travel agents, and picked up any brochures on Paris I could lay my hands on. I'd cut up the travel journals, also stolen from the doctor's surgery. I needed more material for my scrapbook.

I left the travel agents, and walked up the street to Aspen Court, the tower block where I lived. In the forecourt, I removed the sweater, and put it in the bag with the brochures, then I let myself into the building.

The laundrettes were still open, and as I walked past, I could hear the machines roar, and taste the acrid, throat-catching, soap powder. As I looked in, I caught sight of you sitting on a chair, reading. You looked up, and beckoned me in. I walked into the small cream tiled room that housed two large washing machines. I recognised the wicker basket mother used. 'Hello Elly.' You pointed to the basket. 'Your mother was down earlier on.'

'I'll wait till it's finished, Mr Malley.' I sat down next to you. You shut the book and placed it on the other side of your chair, and focused your attention on me. I always thought you'd look more at home strolling through the sunny boulevards of Paris, accordion music straining softly in the background. This was before I even knew you'd been to Paris. You looked every inch the Frenchman abroad, cream chinos, pale blue jerkin, smoky-lenses glasses. It was a shock to hear you speak in a polite, Glaswegian accent.

'How's the French coming on then?' you asked eagerly.

That's why I warmed to you in the first place, you weren't patronising.

'Great.' I told you about the trip to Paris.

'Paris, the greatest city in the world.' You expanded on that, telling me about your time there, after reading Hemingway's *A Moveable Feast*. You'd gone to Paris to write the book you'd been sure was inside you, and how your father wanted you to be a tailor. In Paris you'd written, sewed, and played piano to old silent movies in cinemas.

I'd heard it before, but loved to hear it again, partly for the way – like Bernard – you came alive reliving it all, and you seemed younger. From the tips of your feathery brown hair to the toes of your navy deck shoes, you buzzed with energy. Your machine had lapsed into silence. You unloaded your damp clothes and fed them into a white plastic basket. You walked to the door, then faced me.

'See you next week, Elly,' and you were gone.

My machine was in the final throes of a spin and when it was still, I piled my wet clothes into the wicker basket, with my school bag on top. As I lumbered across the tiled floor, I noticed your book still lying on the ground. Resting my load on the chair, I put it in my school bag and walked to the lifts. No sign of you. I knew your life story but hadn't a clue what floor you stayed on. I decided to hold onto the book till I next saw you.

I took the lift to floor six, then walked to the landing where my door lay ajar. I placed the basket on the hall carpet. From the living room, canned laughter from the TV came on cue. I looked up and saw my mother sitting on the sofa, in her chintzy nightgown, smoking, legs folded up. I slung my bag behind my bedroom door, then hung the wet clothes in the airing cupboard. Suddenly I realised my mother was standing next to me, bloodshot eyes fastened on me.

'You're late,' she accused. 'Have you been dirty, with boys?'

'No,' I continued to hang up the washing, wondering if she's forgotten to take the medication that stopped her thinking that people were trying to poison her milk, and that car headlights were signalling up at her window.

'OK,' she padded down to the kitchen. 'Pies and beans for your tea.'

I finished what I was doing, then went to my room to get out the letter. I took out your book. The cover was a black and white still from a movie – a woman poised, looking up at a tall dark man, smoking. It was stark and dramatic, and the man had a nose like Bernard's.

I read the first page – all-staccato sentences, rapid fire. *Jules and Jim* that's what it was. I remembered seeing it in a documentary late one night. Now I was reading the book itself. Something made me pause. Mother stood next to me again, head lowered, eyes watching me balefully. She caught me off guard, and wrenched the book from my hands. Barely glancing at the back cover, she tore at and ripped the spine from the binding, page by page. Your book was being torn into hundreds of pieces.

'You little whore!' she shouted, '*ménage à trois*, you filthy disgusting little bitch.'

She rushed out to the bin chute and disposed of the loose pages. I followed her. 'That book's not mine!' I shouted. 'It's Mr Malley's!'

She slapped me across the face. 'So he's the propagator of that filth!' She stamped back into the house. Behind a glass panel in the door opposite, a lacy curtain twitched. I followed mother back into the house. She was crying. She slammed the living room door closed so I sat in my room to bide the time.

The smell of baked pie was growing stronger. Then I heard my mother's voice calling me through. She sounded more reasonable now. So I took the letter out of my bag, and carried it through to the kitchen. The smoky kitchen, with its blistering seventies wallpaper and smell of burnt toast, was the most depressing room in the flat. Mother sat opposite, tears dropping onto her beans. I sawed at my brick-hard pie and chewed, and chewed, at the lukewarm beans. When she had finished her dinner, I handed her the letter.

She peered at it. 'What's this?'

I could hardly talk. It was as if someone was pressing on my throat. 'I've been picked to go on the Paris trip.'

She didn't hear me. She opened the envelope, read the letter, sighed, shook her head, then ripped the letter in half.

'After what you've been up to, if you think you're swanning off to Paris when I've not had a holiday for fifteen years, you've got another think coming.'

It always boiled down to this. I felt as though I was playing a game where mother changed the rules when I wasn't looking. I didn't move, couldn't take my eyes off those pieces of white paper, or block out those words. I looked up at her, could see lips moving, but couldn't hear her. I got up and began to walk to my room.

'You wouldn't last five minutes in Paris, lady. You'd end up dead in a bin with a drunk peeing on you. You're too stupid...'

I closed my bedroom door. The Paris brochures stared up at me from the carpet. I retrieved my bag, took out Bernard's sweater, smoothed it out on the bed, then lay down. My head ached.

I fell asleep, waking up when it was much later. Outside I could hear people calling to one another. It was Friday night, the street would be busy all night.

I got up and went through to the living room. The TV was still on, mother lay stretched along the sofa, her legs covered by a greying white hospital blanket. In the flickering light off the screen, I could see she was asleep, her lips moving as she muttered softly. I sat down, took the remote, and turned to the other channels. Friday night was French movie night. It was *Camille Claudel*, a biopic about a sculptress whose mentor was Rodin. I wished I looked like Isabelle Adjani. Bernard would be unable to control himself then.

I watched the love scene – Gérard Depardieu taking her over a table. I watched out of the corner of my eye, should mother wake up but she was in a deep sleep, so I returned my attention to the lovers on television, substituting them for myself and Bernard.

The movie finished, but mother slept on. I crawled on my hands and knees out into the hall, then got to my feet. I slid into mother's room. The windows were open and the room was cool and white. I slipped into her jewellery box and took the money inside. I didn't look to see how much I had until I was safely in my room. By the light of the lamp I saw I had three hundred pounds there. I tucked it under the duvet, and realised I had to act quickly. I emptied out my bag and began to fold clothes, packed a hairbrush and my toothbrush. I laid out clothes to wear next morning, and then got ready for bed as usual.

It was to be the longest night of my life. I lay awake, thinking of what I was going to say to Bernard. I knew he would help me. He was cool, knew how I felt about him – probably felt the same, but just couldn't do anything about it.

I heard the shutters roll up at the newsagents outside, and knew it was six o'clock. I waited a bit, then got up, dressed, made sure the money was safe and slipped into the hall. My mother was still snoring in the living room. With the coast clear I returned to my bedroom, lifted my bag, put on Bernard's sweater, my coat, and crept out of the house. I was able to stop holding my breath now, and went to the lift, pressed the button, and waited.

In the morning silence, the approaching lift sounded loud as it descended to my floor. The door slid back and you were standing there, humming a tune. When you saw me your face creased into a smile. Then you saw my bag and knew something was wrong. But you said, 'Elly, you didn't happen to see the book I left in the laundrette yesterday?'

Head down, I told you what my mother had done. You were angry, but not at me. Then you quizzed me about where I was going. I told you I was staying with Bernard. The lift stopped at the bottom, we got out, and you looked at your watch and told me it was too early to go to see Bernard, and that I shouldn't go on an empty stomach. So you took me to a café, off the main street, and we each demolished a fried breakfast. 'I'm sorry it's not croissants and hot chocolate,' you said. I nodded and drank my hot sweet tea. After the food was gone, we ordered more tea as it was still too early to go anywhere. Around nine-thirty, we paid and left.

We took the bus to Bernard's – the only passengers apart from a baby-faced man, who was still wearing a smart shirt from the night before. His head was in his hands. He was just getting home by the look of him. Outside all was still, as if the trees and houses were holding their breath to see what happened to me. We approached Bernard's house, and got off a stop early. There was someone up and about as we approached, and guitar music floated down from an open window.

You said you'd wait at the outside wall, just to check I was OK. I nodded, then walked up the drive, past Bernard's yellow car. On the porch I rang the doorbell and waited. I turned. You gave me the thumbs up. From behind the door I heard light footsteps approach, and a young woman opened the door and stood there. She was Chinese, and wore a nurse's uniform with white clogs. She looked me up and down. 'Can we help you?'

'I'm looking for Bernard,' I told her. Someone walked towards us from the rear of the house. It was Bernard.

'Elly, *mon dieu*! What are you doing here?' He ushered me in – so far so good. He was pleased to see me. The Chinese nurse wasn't though. Her arms were folded. Bernard showed me into a large sitting room, all blue and white, like sitting in a willow china teapot. We sat down opposite each other. I began to explain what had happened. He shook his head in shock. But he couldn't have been listening after all, because he asked me what I expected him to do.

'Let me stay here.' That was it! I'd said it. But I looked at his face and I had my answer.

'Elly! Are you what, fifteen? I'd be in a lot of trouble if you were to stay here.'

'I thought you cared about me,' I said quietly.

'You are my best student, yes. But that's as far as it goes.' He put his head in his hands. 'I was warned about this sort of thing. I should never have allowed my students to call me Bernard.'

'Take me to Paris with you!' I begged.

He walked over to the window, hands in pockets, 'I'm not going to Paris,' he said quietly. 'I'm going to Hong Kong with my fiancée Ling.'

'I see,' my voice sounded very quiet in the room. I shrank into the chair, trying to make myself invisible. The doorbell sounded through the house. I got up, took off my coat and the jumper. Loud voices came from the hall, then you barged in. You stopped and stared at me and Bernard.

'You're a man!' you accused Bernard.

'Elly!' Bernard turned towards me. 'Why are you doing this? I have only ever been good to you.' He turned back to you. 'What did you expect?'

'I thought *Bernard* was some boy from your class,' you hissed at me. You turned back to Bernard. 'You should be ashamed of yourself, leading on a teenage girl.'

'He won't let me stay,' I said to you. 'He's going to Hong Kong.'

'What do you want to go there for? Paris is the greatest city in the world.'

'You've never lived till you've been to Hong Kong,' Bernard said. You both seemed to have forgotten about me. Up to now I'd enjoyed two men arguing over me. Not for long.

'We'd better be going,' you said. I put my coat on as Bernard took you aside.

'I think you should take your daughter to a psychiatrist,' he said in a low voice. 'She lives in a fantasy world.'

'She's not my daughter. I'm a neighbour,' you replied.

And on that note we left, with him staring after us. At the porch he called out, 'See you on Monday Elly.'

Neither of us replied. We walked down the drive, and down the road. I was trying to think what to do next. You patted my arm, then stopped, struck by some bright idea.

'We can't go to Paris, but we can bring Paris to us.'

'We're in Glasgow.'

'So you live in a fantasy world.' You started to walk fast again, talking just as quickly. 'Sometimes living in a fantasy world is the best thing you can do.' We reached the end of the road. To our right was an underground station. We crossed the street, and went in. You bought two tickets, and we proceeded through the barriers and downstairs. A train had just pulled in. In minutes we were rushing towards our destination, St Enoch Square.

At the top of the steps I half expected to see a METRO sign. I didn't, but when we walked into the daylight, an unfamiliar sight met us. St Enoch Square had been transformed into a large market, red and white striped canopies over all the wares, a hum of voices as customers and traders bought and sold. We wandered around the stalls, admiring small giraffes and pianos twisted out of wire, the smell of hot, baked bread and taste of delicately sliced smoked sausages. We bought two large wild boar sausages, and ate two warm croissants, freshly made. The ones Bernard had given us tasted stale in comparison. Next we tasted volatile pimento mustard, watched as a velvety-voiced man poured hot syrup over a tower of baked apples, inhaled the banked-up piles of fresh cut lavender. I sneaked a cup of sweet wine and you made sure no one saw. We tasted cheeses, cakes, and bit into soft pears –

all sampled with smiles from the traders, and accompanied by the sound of eloquent French.

I was overwhelmed by it all, the variety, and my senses were massaged by all on show. You were in your element, talking in French to all the stallholders, the years peeling back with every new sight, sound, taste and smell.

We must have been there most of the morning, then into early afternoon. We went to the small café area, under large umbrellas, and had coffee with large apple pastries. The waiter was young and blonde, with eyes like a cat's. He smiled over at me a few times, and you said in a low voice that he must fancy me. I made eye contact with him, and received a smile in return.

From our vantage point we could watch the market go on. I could have watched all day, and been smiled at by the waiter, but you had other delights planned. We strolled up Buchanan Street. The sun had come out and violinists busked under the trees. You told me they were playing Saint-Saens. We threw coins into their cases, walked on. We went into the bookstore. I wandered around the shop, then had an idea. I asked an assistant about *Jules and Jim*, and he found it for me. I bought the book and waited for you at the front of the shop.

You came downstairs, and we left the shop. I couldn't wait any longer and pressed the book into your hands. Your face when you saw it! You kissed my cheek, and then we walked up to Sauchiehall Street. You led the way into the arthouse cinema there, as for 'today only' *Cyrano de Bergerac* was playing. Gérard Depardieu looked down from the poster as we went into the foyer. I waited while you bought two tickets, and we went into the small cinema, and sat in the front row.

It was practically empty, apart from a colossal white-haired man who looked like a walrus, and a woman with long black hair and a pale face.

The film started. It was a change to watch a French movie without looking over my shoulder to see if my mother was waking up. When the film finished I wanted to clap. Then we sauntered back into the daylight. Out in Sauchiehall Street you touched my arm. 'We have to go back home Elly,' you told me. 'But you can stay with me just now.'

'Thanks Mr Malley.'

'No more Mr Malley, please. It's Maurice,' you said. We headed for Buchanan Street bus station where we could take a bus straight to Aspen Court.

It began to rain as we got off at our stop, outside the high flats. We walked up to the building, and my head felt light. Luckily no one paid any attention to us.

Then I saw the police car sitting outside. There was a policeman sitting at the wheel. He saw us, held his radio up to his mouth, got out and approached us.

'Can you confirm your name?' he asked me.

I hung my head. 'Elly,' I admitted. 'I can explain everything.'

'I'm sure you can,' the policeman said as he led us into the building. He escorted us to my house. At the door stood a policeman and policewoman, and my mother, still in her nightgown. When she saw you she screamed, 'What have you done to my daughter, you pervert!'

The policewoman tried to calm her. The policeman who escorted us up to the flat stepped forward. 'If you could come downstairs, Mr Malley, for a short interview, while my colleague interviews Elly here.'

'He hasn't done anything wrong!' I shouted, but they ignored me.

'You get in here young lady,' mother shouted at me, and I walked into the house.

The police interviewed me, made me feel dirty, so I can guess what they did to you. It turned out my mother had called the police after she saw that I was gone, and then Bernard called them after we left. They'd put two and two together.

I never saw you again after that. They moved you to another place, and I wasn't allowed to contact you again. I don't care what they say about you. I know the truth.

Apparently you'd never been to Paris at all. You wanted to go, but took a nervous breakdown, and couldn't. You whiled out the years in your father's business, going to evening classes to perfect your French, waiting to go when the time was right. Who knows, maybe you're there now.

Wee Sparra Gets His Wings Clipped

Tony McLean

On the sign outside everyone is cordially invited to *COME IN & ENJOY THE BUZZ.* Inside it's absolutely humming. The smell's a mix of cabbage, chip fat and three-day-old sweat. The place is buzzing alright. The place is the Gala on Hawthorn Street.

Elsie had all her pens and paraphernalia spread out in front of her. A pink pen, a blue one and a green, formed a holy trinity around the school photograph of her granddaughter. Next to that was an image of The Sacred Heart. Her granddaughter was seven. She was seven then but in heaven now. Elsie always brought them to the bingo. They brought her luck. That's what she believed anyway. Everyone in Possil knew the story of Elsie's Wee Shannon.

Wee Shannon smiled up at her granny, her school tie loose around her neck. When the wee soul had brought the photos home her mammy had beat her half to death for having the top button of her shirt loose and her tie all ragged. Elsie touched the photo, stroked The Sacred Heart, and picked up her green pen.

'Game four is any one line. Eyes down! Seven and four, seventy-four. Five and nine, fifty-nine. Three and six, thirty-six. Three and four, thirty-four. Legs eleven.' Elsie listened to the chorus of half-hearted whistles but never pursed her own lips. She dropped her head. Her pen hadn't moved an inch since she'd picked it up. She changed from lucky green to lucky blue, the same colour as Shannon's pullover. She swivelled the pen and lightly tapped the glass frame with it. Her other hand fished in her bag for a Kleenex.

'Ye should buy shares in them Elsie hen,' Betty whispered and touched her on the shoulder.

'Two and seven. Twenty-seven.'

Betty looked at Elsie's cards and reached across to dot the 36 on the middle one. 'You'll win a fortune and never know it.' On her own cards she was waiting on two, three and four. She'd got off to a flyer but was fading.

'On it's own number eight. Eight and four. Eighty-four. One and seven. Seventeen. Tony's den. Number t...'

The chorus of boos was interrupted by Betty shouting hysterically. 'HOUSE!' she bellowed, her hand waving from side to side in the air. 'Woo! See that Elsie. Forty quid.'

'House called. Check please.'

Elsie looked at the smiling Betty through glazed eyes. 'That was ma Wee Shannon that done that,' she whimpered. 'She's lookin doon oan her granny and her pals awright.' She touched Shannon's face.

Betty managed a sympathetic smile for her friend.

*

Sparra swaggered down the Fountainwell Road whistling *The Sash*. His hands moved rhythmically by his side. In his mind he was on The Walk, birling a baton or pounding on a drum. Either way, he was playing a major part in the parade. He was stoned out his thruppneys. He pulled his keys from his pocket and threw them in the air. When they dropped he caught them and passed them from his right hand to his left behind his back. He did this a couple of times until he eventually looked as though he was playing with an invisible hula hoop. He stopped still and held the key ring in front of his face, looking for his whistle. He grabbed it, placed it to his lips and started blowing what he thought to be *Rule Britannia*. It was nothing like it, just a high-pitched wail. He reached the bus stop and put the key ring – whistle and all – into his pocket. He looked through the graffiti and plastic to the inside of the bus shelter. There was a couple his age propped together in the far corner. He was sure he recognised the guy. He held back though. That sort of fake recognition thing happened a lot when he'd indulged. He looked again. He did recognise him, but couldn't remember where from. He scoured his mind and his memories went on a helter-skelter ride through the years until he hit the right memory. God! Ten years ago, Barmulloch, Big Alan McKinley. Sparra went into the shelter.

'Alan! How ye doin pal?' Wee Sparra slapped the big guy on the shoulder and held out his hand to shake. The couple looked at him. They were completely guttered – been on the piss all day – and unable at first to focus. 'It's Wee Sparra, Alan. Ye must remember me. Used tae run aboot Barmulloch thegither. Remember?'

'Naw.' Alan railed against the plastic of the shelter and grabbed Sparra by the zip of his jacket. 'Ah'rr don't remember.' The big fella's speech was gone and his legs were just about to follow suit. His girlfriend had already taken advantage of the seating facilities.

'Kin we no git a taxi?' she drawled. 'C'mon Alan.'

Alan was busy trying to focus on the wee guy in front of him.

'C'mon,' Sparra jumped up and down excitedly. If he could've, he'd've flapped his wings. 'Ye must remember me.' He smiled straight at the big guy's face. 'Sparra?' He cocked his head to one side chirpily.

BINGO! Alan's eyes registered CLUNK
CLUNK
CLUNK £ £ £.
Fruit-machine style the cogs of his mind clicked into place. He'd waited years for this and grabbed Sparra's jacket tighter. 'Aye Ah fuckin remember ye,' he screamed. 'Ah did six fuckin year fur ye ya grassin wee prick!' He moved Sparra round and banged him savagely against the shelter, causing his head to knock on the metal divider.

'Whit ye daein Alan?' His girlfriend screamed. 'Leave um! Leave um!' She pulled at Alan's arms getting in-between the two men. Alan reluctantly released his grip.

'Ye've got the wrang guy Alan. That wisnae me. Ah didnae grass oan ye big chap. Ye know me? Ah widnae dae that.'

Alan fell back against the plastic and sat on the seat. His mind blurred and focused, blurred and finally focused with clarity. He got up and walked towards Sparra. As he was within two feet he lost it again. 'Ye fuckin did ya…' He lunged at him and fell flat on his face.

Sparra ran a few steps backwards. 'That's right ya big prick!' He waved his arms taunting Alan. 'Ah grassed ye. C'mon ya dick. Anytime.' Sparra thought he was safe, but Alan got up and leapt once more towards him. He turned on his heels and ran round in circles. This would be so easy, he thought. The big fella's completely fucked. As he ran he looked over his shoulder. Alan's legs were doing an unnatural impersonation of the sails on a windmill. His torso joined in, lurching forward in violent spasms. He was like some ghostly drunken phantom. Amazingly, he didn't fall over, but somehow managed to stagger against the plastic of the shelter.

'Linda,' he slurred. 'That's that bastard Ah told ye aboot. That fuckin Sparra. Gie me that knife.'

'Who? Whit knife?' Linda didn't have a clue what was happening at all and watching Alan run around in circles was making her feel ill.

'The knife.' Alan held out his hand and winked at her way too deliberately. 'Ye know,' wink wink, 'the knife, the knife.'

'We don't have a knife.' Even the conversation was making her feel ill.

Alan pressed his fingers to his lips. 'Sshh.' He started running again.

Linda slumped all over the seat, her head facing the ground in case she chucked. 'Ah don't know whit ye're talkin aboot, Alan. Stoap runnin aboot wid ye?' He did. He fell flat on his face in the road.

Sparra had completely forgotten about what he'd done to Big Alan. Jeezo, it was a lump of a thing to forget. He was enjoying himself though, having remembered how gormless the big chap was. He looked over his shoulder and saw Alan slumped on the road. He walked over and laughed into the back of his head. 'Ye always wur a bit slow Al,' he chirped. 'Ye should've got yerself in trainin while ye wur banged up.' Sparra bent over and ruffled the big man's hair. 'See ya sucker.' He flew towards the taxi that had just pulled up at the rank.

Alan grunted on the wet ground and tried to raise himself to his pins. As he did so **B E E P! B E E P!** the driver of the bus behind him stared and shook his head. He was lucky to have spotted him. Alan rose as though from the dead and held his hands against the windscreen. He felt his way round to the doors of the vehicle and as he stood at the open doors he made a supreme effort to lift himself onto the bus. He grabbed hold of the handrail next to the driver's seat and pointed at the road ahead. 'Follow that taxi!' he instructed the driver.

The driver looked at him; he'd heard it all now. 'Where ye gaun pal?' the driver asked.

'Follow that taxi!' Alan repeated. The taxi was now round the corner and out of sight.

'Listen pal,' the driver sighed. 'If ye don't put any money in there we're followin nothin.' He pointed at the flaking red moneybox.

'Follow that taxi!'

'Money in the box!'

'Follow that ta...' Alan fished in his pocket for money.

'Money!' The driver growled. 'Or get aff!'

Alan fired a random coin into the slot and his eyes asked the driver for a ticket.

'Where ye gaun?' the driver asked.

'Follow that taxi!'

'For five pence?' The driver laughed. 'Try again.'

Alan once more fished in his pocket but was distracted by some shouting behind him. 'Alan? Where ye gaun? That's no oor bus. We want a forty-five, that's an eighty-nine.' Linda groaned at him from her prone position. Alan eventually found a heavy coin and threw it into the slot. It was a pound coin and the machine spewed a ticket out for him. The bus pulled away from the stop and Linda stared at the back of it before letting her head fall once more against the metal of the bus shelter seat.

'Will you sit doon?' The driver instructed Alan. He never answered, just burped and slammed into the fire extinguisher. He fell onto the luggage rack.

'Sit doon!' the driver shouted again.

'Ah um sittin doon,' Alan slurred back.

*

Elsie slipped another cigarette from her box and picked up the lighter from the table. With her other hand she delved in her bag for the half bottle. She'd bought a Coke from the bar at the start of the night but since then she'd been dipping in and out of her bag for the half bottle and the big bottle of Savers' cola. Everybody did the same and the folk that ran the bingo hall knew it. They were smarter than to do anything about it though. She looked at Betty's glass. 'Ye wantin another wan?' she asked.

Betty didn't even need to look at Elsie to know she was pished again. Every Monday, Wednesday and Sunday it was the same, vodka-diluted tears.

'It wid've been her birthday next week,' Elsie sniffed and wiped at her eyes. Betty nodded. It might well have been her birthday next week, but Elsie had said the same thing the week before and the week before that... Four vodkas in meant there was always a birthday coming up. Betty understood the sorrowful paths that grief could take you down, but by Christ it was difficult keeping up. Ten years down the line she'd more counselling skills than she really needed.

'Come on Elsie love, try an' concentrate,' Betty patted her shoulder.

'Ladies. Any minute now we're crossing over to join Gala bingo halls throughout the country for The National. This is the final game on the card, number...'

*

Sparra was sure he was safe. Big tube couldn't catch cold, never mind a fly-boy like himself. The taxi rolled on down the Springburn end of Hawthorn Street and stopped at the traffic lights just past the railway bridge. He knew he hadn't enough for the taxi fare. He'd had to leave the pub because he couldn't afford a pint for Christ's sake! He'd about a pound in shrapnel in his pocket and the meter was nearly up to four quid. He'd have to pick his moment. These new taxis with their central locking were a bugger to do a runner from. The lights changed to green and the taxi chugged on past the Ashfield Club, the floodlights from the greyhound racing illuminating the dark sky.

'We're hauvin nae luck wi the lights the night ur we?' the driver shouted through the gap as the taxi came to a halt at the junction by the old Possil bus garage.

'Always the same,' Sparra replied, trying to pull down the window. It never budged. Another feature of these new taxis. The driver looked at him in the mirror and The Bold Boy tried his best not to catch his eye. 'Any chance ey windin the windae doon? Ah've a big greener Ah need rid ey.' The driver screwed up his face and pressed a button on his dashboard.

Incredibly, the bus, whose luggage rack Alan was sprawled over, was just trundling under the railway bridge on Hawthorn Street. He got to his feet and held on to the rail by the driver's door. 'C'moan!' he encouraged. 'Get the fit doon big chap.' They swept through the lights as they were about to change and Alan whooped with delight. 'Yee Ha!' The double-decker was flat out as it passed the Ashfield. Alan peered through the rain at the road ahead. He spotted a taxi stopped at the next set of traffic lights and wondered if it was the one he was after.

Sparra put both his head and his hands through the open

window. His hand reached for the handle and turned. The door sprang open at the same time as he cleared his throat. He let out a phlegm-filled rasp that distracted the driver's attention and both his feet splashed into a puddle. He was off and running.

The driver looked over his shoulder and saw Sparra had bolted. 'Ah thought ye were gaun tae Maryhi... Jesus!' He was getting too old for this. The lights were still at red so he opened the cab door and made to get out.

'That's him!' Alan shrieked excitedly. 'That's him.' Thirty yards ahead he could see Sparra legging it from the taxi. Alan pulled open the driver's cab and shouted at him. 'C'mon. We've got him noo.' He reached across in front of the driver and beeped the horn on the steering wheel. The driver turned and faced him. 'Fur God's sake man!' he shouted. 'Whit the hell ye tryin tae dae? Ye'll cause an acc…'

BANG!

The bus drove straight into the back of the taxi just as the driver had got out of the door. He looked on impotently as the speeding double-decker pushed his black cab fifteen feet into the middle of the box junction. He covered his eyes as another bus – a single-decker, with the lights and the right of way – crashed into the side of his cab. He just stood there, unsure of whether he should be happy to be alive or angry that his livelihood had all of a sudden gone for a Burton. He saw Sparra run across the road and through the gate into the bingo car park. He got his overweight body into gear and gave chase.

Alan fell on the floor of the bus and was relieved when it came to a halt. The sound of the crunch had scared him, almost to the point of sobering up. Not quite though. He clawed his way to his feet and stood theatrically dusting himself down. The bus was filled with noisy babbling passengers thanking their lucky stars and 'Oh my God!'ing all over the shop.

'Ya big bloody tube!' The driver shouted at him. 'We could've aw been fuckin killed there!'

Alan looked ahead as Sparra ran around the bingo car park while an irate fat guy at the gate shook a comedy fist at him. 'Kin ye open the door?' he asked the bus driver.

'Not a chance,' The driver replied. 'You're waitin here. This is aw your faul…'

Before he'd finished speaking Alan reached up and pressed the Emergency Exit button. The door whooshed open and he whooshed out. His legs were jelly, and as soon as his feet hit the concrete of the pavement his face did the same. He lay there, and with his cheek resting in a puddle, considered how much he'd suffered. He'd taken all the doins in the nick for the sneaky wee shite – his feathered friend who'd got off on a technicality. Scot-free. Sure, it'd been Sparra's face that had decorated the front pages for a couple of days. A few days shame was all that git had to contend with. Alan, however, had the shame *and* the beatings for the first three years. Life smiled on some people. Alan wasn't some people. With his hands palm-down in the puddle he picked himself up off the ground. He shook his head from side to side and started running across the road towards the bingo. He wasn't paying the greatest amount of attention and was surprised when a car, slowing down to look at the accident, caught the tail of his coat as it flapped behind. It was going at such a speed, however, that it would hardly have dented his pride. It was a warning nonetheless. He wiped his eyes and peered at the dot in the distance that was Sparra.

Sparra looked around and saw a trail of people running after him. The taxi driver was being overtaken by Alan, who in turn was being chased by a bus driver, who himself was being pursued by another bus driver. Disney comes to Possil! He looked around for options. The fence that surrounded the car park was too high for him to leap, or even climb, and his only other means of escape was back the way he'd came. That particular route was covered by Alan, the taxi driver, two bus drivers *and* Uncle Tom Cobley an all. He'd have to go inside, try and lose them in there.

The warm air fans that rested above the doors to the Gala almost blew him away. For a moment he forgot that he was being hounded by a seemingly ever-expanding posse and stood still. The air was good; it calmed him, swept over his face like a velvet chamois and made him feel about three years old again. Life was... Oh Shit! Another look over the shoulder and the running started again. He moved invisibly past recalcitrant staff in badly ironed uniforms, swished by the plaque of Excellence to Service, went through one set of double doors, up some stairs and then through a second set of double doors. BINGO!

Oh my God! He stood for a second and stared at a sea of pink and blue-rinsed barnets. *Voyage of the Damned* had nothing on this scene. His mind was shocked, not by the hairstyles, but by the silence. A pin dropping would have deafened him. He was all too aware of his own breath, the heavy, hot wheezing over which he had no control. His exertions had taken their toll.

'Take a seat at the back please.' A voice came from the

wilderness at the front of the hall. Whoever it was looked like an insignificant blip next to the over-sized cinema screen he stood in front of. 'Best of order during The National.'

A couple of hundred women, made up like Hallowe'en cakes, turned and stared at him. All he could see were faces covered in white powder splashed by rouge-red cheeks. He started laughing. This was too freaky.

'Take a seat please.' The voice in the wilderness ordered once more. 'The National's about to begin.'

Sparra shuffled uncomfortably, turned and opened the double doors he'd come through. He quickly closed them over again when he saw the posse on the stairs heading his way.

'Could you take a seat please.'

Sparra looked to the front and a massive head appeared on the screen. 'Good evening ladies and gentlemen. Eyes down for The National. The first ball. Five and sev...'

The doors behind Sparra burst open and he sprung into life. He hurdled the first table without a hitch and landed running. Behind him the posse stood puffing, panting and planning their strategy. The taxi driver acted as sheriff and pointed his deputies in different directions. They dispersed just as Sparra was vaulting a double table. His front leg met the ground fine but his trailing one clattered against a bottle of soda water and he fell awkwardly. He quickly got to his feet and looked around. The sea of Hallowe'en cakes still stared. Pandemonium ensued.

'Security! Security!' The voice in the wilderness cried.

'One and seven. Sevente...'

'Whit'd he say?

'Whit wis that?'

'Wis that seventy?'

Sparra bounded from table to table, scattering and spilling glasses as he did. He saw the green neon of an EXIT in the distance and made for it. From table to table he bounded like some stubby gazelle. Things were going too well. Far too well. He'd done four tables on the trot now and as he leapt to his fifth he looked around. He should've kept his eyes on the road. His trainer landed on something glassy and sent his body spinning. He landed on the table back first. 'Fuck!' he groaned. The stuffing had been knocked from him and his wings no longer had the desire to fly.

He had landed on Wee Shannon's photograph and had snapped the frame.

Elsie looked through her teary eyes at the figure that had landed out of the sky. The figure that now held the Sacred Heart in his hand and was staring at it quizzically. She wiped her eyes and looked again.

'It's him!' she squealed. 'The joy rider.' The shock too much for her addled mind.

Beside her, Betty had fallen backwards from her seat at the sight of the oncoming Sparra.

'It's him!' she squealed again. 'The bastard that killed ma Shannon!'

Betty got to her feet slowly, her hip feeling as though it had snapped in two.

'Who?' she asked. 'Him?'

Elsie got to her feet and started beating Sparra on the chest. 'Ya bastard! Ya wee bastard!' A crowd was gathering round her, the original posse stuck at the back, bouncing up and down to get a view of proceedings.

Sparra felt as though he'd been paralysed. He could feel nothing from the neck down. 'Wait a minute missus,' he pleaded. 'Haud yer hoarses!'

Elsie shuffled her hands over the table and grabbed a large shard of glass from the table and held it over Sparra's throat. 'Ah'll kill ye! Ma wee Shannon. You killed ma wee Shannon!' Her voice was as weak as water, she'd no energy left to fight and instead of plunging the glass into Sparra's flesh she threw it to the floor. 'But that's whit ye want. That brings me doon tae your level.'

'Good tae see ye're seein sense missus.' In his mind Sparra was swaggering again, back on The Walk. 'Ye don't want tae dae anythin daft.'

Betty looked at her pal. After all these years. All the tears, the grief, the heartache and counselling. All the years she had propped poor Elsie up. She didn't want to think anymore and picked up a piece of the shattered photo frame.

She went for Sparra and the feathers flew.

Fair Friday

Kenny Manley

Rab eased back the curtain and surveyed the scene through a bleary eye.

Rain teemed down incessantly from a gloomy, grey-white sky, and by the look of the tenements opposite, it had been pouring down for quite some time. Veins of water flowed from the gutters down the sandstone façades, spreading out like deltas leaving the lower half of the building one huge wall of dampness. Scars and blemishes created by the water looked almost painful as they gaped at the elements. Windows looked down appalled by the pitiful state, while the slated roof had turned depressingly black as if it mourned its own demise. Glasgow certainly didn't look miles better when it rained.

Typical start to the Glasgow Fair fortnight. Or was it? To be honest Rab couldn't really remember the weather from one year to the next on this particular day. One thing he was sure of though was that every pessimist in town would be on the streets assuring all and sundry that it always rained on Fair Friday, even if it didn't. Glaswegians reckoned the heavens had a definite grudge against them, especially when it came to holidays.

Rab yawned intensely, letting the curtain go and moved uneasily back towards his bed through the assorted debris that littered the floor. He sat on the edge in the semi-darkness considering the day ahead.

Fair Friday. Normally a time for celebration. The start of the summer holidays for most folk in Glasgow, if you worked that is, and if you didn't, well, just another boring day.

Beginning of February he had been laid off. Six bloody months on the dole. It seemed longer, much longer. Closure of the factory had come as a shock, a complete bombshell. Rab had been shattered.

For months beforehand there had been rumour and counter rumour, nothing definite. Then came that fateful morning when management had called a meeting at the workplace. The workers had stood in disbelief as they were given a diatribe on 'World Recession', and 'Unfavourable Economic Conditions', followed by an announcement that the plant would be closed within the month. Two weeks into the New Year, all the best and here's your P45. So here he was July 13th and still no sign of a job.

He wondered what time it was. He'd lost track recently as his days and nights had become more and more irregular. His watch lay redundant on the small table by the bed. The battery had gone flat several weeks beforehand, but there was no question of a replacement. That would be an extravagance to say the least in his present financial situation. Essentials only and to hell with everything else. OK, maybe a few pints with the boys the weekend after he'd received his Giro. A pittance of a social life, but it was better than none. If anything, it helped to keep his sanity in an insane existence.

Rab had realised early on the need to change his lifestyle from being a free-spending type, to someone who was always looking for discounts or, even better, something for nothing. He was also aware that unemployment could quickly become a way of life with no hope of escape. You only had to go as far as the huge housing schemes on the periphery of the city to witness a subculture based on the hopelessness and despair of the benefit dependency. Potential employers were only too aware of this problem and were reluctant to waste time or money on what they considered 'work-shy' people.

Every day Rab was finding it more and more difficult to motivate himself. He knew the longer he remained unemployed, the harder it would be to find work.

So what would he do today? The idea of curling back under the sheets was very inviting. Lying all day and night just dozing and dreaming. Declare Fair Friday a non-day, miss it out completely. Apart from anything else just think of the food he could save. A possible six slices of bread. A tin of beans or soup, definitely not both. A fair size piece of cheese. Maybe three tea bags and up to half a pint of milk. Come Saturday he could be positively gluttonous feasting on the surplus. Certainly worth staying in bed for.

So what was the alternative? Out and about? Where would he go? Should be just go out and let his feet make the decision, even if it meant wandering around aimlessly for half an hour getting drenched. He had to see other people. Share experiences, even if it was only a wet raincoat. His brain would soon stagnate, cells rot away if he started lying in his bed day after day. Inane conversation was better than none and there was always the weather to discuss, that infinite topic of conversation in Glasgow on a day like this.

Standing up, a sudden sense of purpose coming over him. He was going out, of that he was now sure. So where? The pub was ruled out for obvious reasons. The library, overdue books.

Art galleries? Too far, couldn't afford a bus. Job Centre?

Job Centre! That was it. Not too far, hadn't been down for a couple of weeks. Might even get a job. Never know, it's happened before. So he'd been told.

Immediately a vision of the local Job Centre was conjured up in his mind, but this time it was utterly distinct from the norm. Stands and boards overflowed with jobs, and not just any jobs. Real jobs, specifically designed for his needs. Well paid, company car, no qualifications or experience required, must be six months unemployed. Smiling, enthusiastic staff glided majestically from person to person with fistfuls of workcards encouraging people, actively forcing people, to apply.

Snapping out of his dream he began to rummage through the heaps of clothes strewn along the length of his couch. Some were filthy, to say the least, and smelt of sweat and damp. But not everything was dirty, and laundry day was one a month when everything would be quite foul.

He slipped into his cleanest pair of jeans and the freshest looking sweatshirt. Both of which seemed over-generous in size. Whether this was due to stretching or lack of decent meals he couldn't really pinpoint.

Breakfast was given a by, as had been normal practice in recent weeks and he was soon out on the street, rain bouncing off his forehead, running down his face. He huddled deeper into his raincoat, feeling he was going to regret this excursion.

'A quarter past twelve,' replied the tall, thin gentleman from the safety of the bus shelter.

Quarter past twelve, thought Rab, as he hurried up the road. Not bad. Not bad at all, going by recent standards.

Five minutes into his walk and he was beginning to wish he had declared today a non-day after all. Why had he left the luxury of his flat? he asked himself, as the rain continued to batter down. His raincoat was soon completely sodden, the lower half of his jeans sticking to his legs, like clingfilm round an old cheese roll. A cold would be inevitable, just the tonic he needed.

Rab upped the pace and soon found himself in an unhealthy jog, his body hunched forward uncomfortably, head bowed, raising his eyes only occasionally in case someone else was doing the same thing from the opposite direction.

Heavy traffic droned by in both directions, their tyres swishing as they soaked up the ample surface water. Up ahead a car broke ranks, its indicator light flashing furiously as it drew towards the kerb. Rab didn't take much notice, not knowing many people on the Southside. He jogged, half trudged past without as much as a glance. Even so a feeling of uneasiness crept over him on passing the stationary vehicle as if being watched from within. Then came the whine of the automatic window being lowered, followed by a faint, almost inaudible cry. Again, this time louder, more positive.

'Rab!'

Rab swung round, pulling his collar up for the umpteenth time, peering at the car inquisitively. Half sprawled across the passenger seat lay the driver, the sole occupant grinning madly at the open window.

'Rab, how are you?' said a rather posh, unfamiliar voice.

But the face, he knew the face. Take away the moustache. Name? What's the guy's name again? Lived up the same street in the scheme. He stalled for a couple of seconds expressing facial recognition, hoping the guy would introduce himself.

'It's me, Gordon Hamilton. Lived up the same street!'

'Gordon bloody Hamilton, that's it,' he murmured discreetly. 'How ye doin Gordon? Sorry, I just couldnae remember your name there. Last guy in the world I was expectin' tae see today.'

'Oh don't worry about that Rab, it's been a long time. Wouldn't expect you to recognise me immediately. So, how are you keeping yourself?'

'Fine Gordon, just fine,' Rab blurted out convincingly.

'I have to admit, Rab you're not looking too good, if you don't mind me saying.'

Rab stood staring at the ground like a schoolboy up before the headmaster for some minor misdemeanour.

Maybe it was the accent that made him feel that way. Gordon had always fancied himself for sure, but he'd always talked the same as the rest of them.

No point in Rab putting on a pretence, he was hardly going to fool our Gordon with his new voice, new face, suit and fancy car.

'Could be worse Gordon, but not much worse,' he said fingering nervously at his collar.

'Well the least I can do is give you a lift, jump in.'

Rab clambered into the car somewhat awkwardly as if trying to minimise the inevitable soaking of the passenger seat.

'Must say Gordon, you look as if you're doin' pretty well for yourself.'

'I'm doing fine, thanks. Running my own Management Consultancy Business. It's great being your own boss, it's really such a tremendous challenge. You should seriously consider it yourself, all you need is a few grand to get the ball rolling.'

'Aye Gordon, I might just do that. Maybe run a wee firm advising people how to survive on forty quid a week.'

'You're not unemployed, surely not?' said Gordon as if coming in contact with a new species that he'd only heard about in the papers or on television.

'Fraid so Gordon. Got the big heave way back in February.'

'Really, whatever happened?'

'Closure, Thruston Electrics?'

'Oh yes, I think I remember now, wasn't viable or something.'

Rab look at Gordon.

'Wiznae bloody viable! Well I can tell you Gordon. It's bloody viable now alright! Sweatshops of Brazil, that's where they make their components now!'

'It's a competitive market out there. If Thruston don't go to Brazil, someone else will.'

'Don't give me yer competitive market nonsense! I'll tell ye what it is Gordon! Slave market, bloody slave market! Nothing more, nothing less. A company that would rather employ cheap labour in Brazil than us. Puttin' their own countrymen on the dole for the sake of maximising profit, 'cause don't tell me they weren't making a profit in Glasgow!'

'Steady on Rab, steady on. I was just being a realist. No one likes to see one of the lads unemployed.'

Rab gave a sardonic laugh. Gordon one of the lads indeed.

'Well where can I drop you?' said Gordon after a few moments' embarrassing silence.

Rab sat motionless, his gaze unable to penetrate the blurred windscreen. He was feeling uncomfortable at accepting a lift from someone whose jaw he would dearly like to crack at this particular moment. The alternative was to swallow his pride and save himself an extra ten-minute drenching.

'Job Centre, straight down the road.'

Gordon soon manoeuvred the car into the stream of traffic heading south.

Rab admired the plush interior of the car, keeping his thoughts to himself. Gordon had certainly come a long way since their teenage days up in the scheme. Twenty years ago he couldn't even run a game of cards in the street, now here he was advising people how to run their firms. Life was certainly full of surprises.

'So wher ye stayin' these days?' said Rab as they drew to a halt at the traffic lights.

'Up by Eastwood Toll, you really should come up some time.'

'Oh aye. Eastwood Toll, very fancy. Ever back up by?'

'You mean back up the scheme?' said Gordon with a look of horror on his face.

'Aye,' said Rab prompting an answer.

'Can't say I am.'

'What about your family, friends, surely you keep in touch?'

'Haven't much in common nowadays.'

'Don't suppose ye will if ye never go up and see them. You one of the lads as well.'

'Look Rab, don't start moralising! We both came from the scheme, that's all in the past. It's up to us to better ourselves as individuals and forget about that God-Forsaken dump!'

'God-forsaken dump! That God-Forsaken dump was your home whether you like it or not!'

'Give me a break will you. I don't want to discuss the past. The future and where I'm going in life is what concerns me now, and I'm certainly not going to get all sentimental about things that happened over twenty years ago!'

'OK, OK. Keep the heid. I just didnae think that a wee dunderheid like you would end up bein' ashamed of yer past.'

'Oh fuck off!'

'Oh aye, well at least ye still know how tae swear, ye canny have forgotten everything. Or is this part of your new Management Consultancy style?'

There was no attempt to respond, the lights were green and Gordon was too busy looking for the Job Centre in the array of offices, pubs, restaurants and shops which cluttered either side of the road beyond the crossroads.

'There it is,' said Rab a few seconds drive later. 'Anywhere around about here will do fine.'

Gordon's reaction was immediate, swinging the car into a tight space causing the driver behind some consternation, resulting in a few angry blasts from his horn.

'Friends of yours Gordon?' Rab queried sarcastically. 'Well thanks for the lift.' He took a last glance at Gordon, his calm, assured features replaced by a tense, strained, crumpled-looking face behind the wheel.

Gordon was growing impatient with both the departing passenger and the surrounding traffic. Rab slammed the door shut, relieved to be rid of his good Samaritan.

Rain and reality quickly reasserted themselves as a frenzy of people splashed about the battered, cracked, puddly pavement. Some shrouded deep within waterproofs. Others, umbrellas bobbing aloft, defiantly deflecting the downpour.

Meanwhile shopping trolleys bundled with plastic bags meandered along, pushed by raincoats and hats. The less fortunate exposed to the lashing torrents.

But not to worry. There it was. Grey metal grating covered the large expanse of glass, punctuated by the outline of two smooth, steel framed, swing doors. A huge unpretentious sign above in ghastly orange and black declaring bluntly 'JOB CENTRE.' Hardly an inspiring sight, but nonetheless welcome.

Soon his hands were grasping at the handles pushing then pulling. Both doors. No movement. Again, in disbelief. Solid. Momentarily confused he gazed at the door oblivious to the water running down his neck. Gradually his eyes focused through the mesh on a notice staring indifferently back:

'THIS JOB CENTRE WILL BE CLOSED ON FRIDAY 13TH JULY AND MONDAY 16TH JULY FOR GLASGOW FAIR HOLIDAY.'

The Park Bench

Roberta McLennan

The scene is set. Laid out before you is a carpet of lush grass. It is early summer. The sun is piercing like shards of glass reflecting through the gaps of the tall trees: birch, pine and oak. The birdsong is muted by the happy cries of children playing, skipping and cycling. Spread out on the grass are little groups of families picnicking, the occasional solitary figure reading, entwined lovers, people sitting on the park benches. Kite ribbons are fluttering in the air, and their bright colours catch your eye as they stream by. People walking on the well-marked paths politely nod to others as they pass.

Taking an overhead view we glimpse winding grey paths leading us to the tennis courts, the bowling green, the pond, the children's corner and up, up to the top. Circling the hill like a crown are the trees with their many hues of green, and a sprinkling of gold. Edging the crown is the beetroot-coloured copper beech. On pushing aside the leaves of the copper beech, which has been allowed to expand and stretch, we discover a gate. Opening the gate, we find a sunken garden. Carefully stepping down the six stairs we see that only one bench has escaped the vandals.

The concrete walls are looking their age and the ragged plants still clinging to their surface only add to the dejection. The overhanging branches of slumped trees form a shadowy ceiling. Where once flowerbeds were neatly set out, a few roses and fuchsias flourish. It is as if they are saying, 'Here we are and here we will stay.'

Since her mother died five years ago, Janice Abbot has

come here every Saturday morning. It is a sort of memorial to happier days, when Janice brought her mother here; when the garden was sunnier and the local council spent time and money on this hidden part of the park. It is the most unlikely of meeting places.

We notice that Janice's face lights up at the approach of an elderly gentleman. This place holds special memories for him too: he used to come with his wife Elsie, who died a few months before Mrs Abbot. His name is Hughie Walsh. He is a kind man in his sixties, and is only too aware of Janice's retiring nature. It took him a year to get more than a perfunctory greeting out of Janice, and another year before he could persuade her to go with him for a cup of tea.

'So you've have come then?'

'Aye lass.'

Hughie sits down on the bench, and is silent for a moment. He is gathering his breath. He turns to Janice and holds her two hands in his.

'I don't think we should meet here anymore.'

Janice's face droops and her shoulders heave and collapse. You can hear her think, 'I didn't realise how much he means to me until now.'

'Janice, you have not been listening. Have you heard a word that I have been saying?' The reply is a glazed look. Janice is fighting hard not to cry.

'I was saying Janice, we have to look forward. No more looking back. You'll be retiring in a few weeks time. Have you given any thought to your future?'

Hughie's voice fades into a foggy background. Janice hears another voice. Listen closely: it is her mother's whining tone.

'Janice Abbot I worry about you. How will you mange when I'm gone? Girl, you lack any sort of initiative and drive.'

You can feel her new-found confidence evaporating like mist. This man has given her so much: friendship, self-esteem and love. She is coming out of her stupor and begins to catch his words. She looks at Hughie. His face is anxious.

'What?'

Something is nudging her fingers. She looks down and sees a little green velvet box.

Hughie tenderly wipes away her tears.

'Lass, I'm asking you to marry me.'

We will leave them there and quietly tiptoe up the steps and gently push back the copper beech leaves shielding their secrets.

The Bunnet

Anne Maley

James whistled cheerily as he stirred the tea. Saturday morning! He liked weekends, nae weans! Oh he was fond of his grandchildren, but didn't he see them every weekday? He fetched them from the other side of the council estate and delivered them to the primary school near his cottage home. Their mothers, his youngest daughters, went out to work. When they first started school Grandma marched them back and forth and hovered at playtime lest her darlings be bullied. She soon realised that this was unnecessary. Norma, aged five, was quite capable of defending herself and her less aggressive cousin. The only person allowed to bully him was his tumchie relative.

So James was in a happy mood as he carried the tea ben the room. His wife sat up in bed and sipped her tea, smiling at the thought of the day ahead. Shopping with the girls. James turned on the radio to get the news.

'Mind you promised to look after the weans today.'

He almost dropped his cup! Last week's kindly offer had slipped his mind. His wife and daughters were shopping today to buy a present and outfits to wear at a family wedding. His heart sank, nae fitba' this afternoon. However, not one to brood over minor disappointments, he planned his day out with his grandchildren.

'I'll take them to the Barras. I want to see Harry, to ask if he can fix my watch. Then we'll go to the Green and the People's Palace. The weans enjoy the museum.'

'The Barras are always so crowded, mind you don't lose them. And keep a firm grip on that wee Norma... I don't think you should bother with that old watch. You have the one Tim gave you for your birthday.'

James looked at the old watch and put it carefully in his pocket. 'This watch is special. Oor Jimmy made this one at college when he did that horology course.'

'That was years ago, James, maybe the watch is finished.'

Anne went to the window to look out for the family. Here come the weans, running ahead as usual. They burst through the back door, running round Granda's chair, scattering his newspaper to the floor. 'I won,' said the boy, bravely. 'You shoved me at the gate!' said his fiery cousin, face flushed, hair wind blown, ribbons askew. She was about to attack Sonny when Granda rose to referee the pair. 'Noo' behave or I'll no' take you to the Barras.'

'Oh Granda, we'll be good.' She threw herself at him and he sat down suddenly and found himself on the receiving end of a bear hug.

The boy retrieved the scattered pages of the newspaper, and joined his cousin on Granda's knee. 'Help!' cried James, 'you'll have me through the bottom of this chair.'

However, their youthful enthusiasm affected James and he walked with jaunty step towards the bus stop. He smiled fondly on the two as they romped down the road ahead. Holding hands, knees almost touching chins, skipping in joyful abandon!

He had the first vague misgivings about the outing when they were stuck in the usual traffic jam in Union Street. They sat at the back of the crowded bus, Sonny squashed in the corner, Norma on Granda's knee. Everyone getting bored, peering out the steamed up, manky, windows. Suddenly the driver's voice boomed up the bus. 'Don't touch that sonny!'

Heads swivelled. James looked at his footerie fingered grandson, who sat, arms folded, a faraway look on his cherubic features. Norma leaned over and fixed her cousin with a steady stare.

He scarcely blinked, maintaining his bland innocent expression. Heads swivelled once more as Norma wanted to know, in a hoarse stage whisper, that carried the length of the bus, how did the driver know Sonny's name? Two lassies sitting across the passage, giggled, and Norma glared. Sonny gazed into space, unruffled.

Off the bus, Granda wanted to know, 'Did you touch the emergency door handle?'

Sonny, wearing injured expression, 'Naw!'

Norma danced round him, 'He did, he did!'

In an instant the pair were locked in battle.

Granda took a firm grip of the small pugilists. 'Right,' he said, 'forward march, save your energy for the walking we have to do.'

A wonderful place the big open market. The children loved the bustle and noise, they lost Granda twice. He looked very pleased when they found him again! Everyone seemed happy and cheerful, a sunny day, after weeks of rain. The stallholders cracking daft jokes as they extolled the value of their wares.

James took a firm grip of his charges and headed for Harry's stall. They liked this, and were soon behind his counter.

Sonny's footerie fingers getting into Harry's precious accoutrements. Granda gave them some money and they galloped off through the crowds to the stall with the toys and games.

The two old friends discussed the coming family wedding while Harry worked on the watch, and went on to talking about Celtic's chance of winning the cup.

James was just beginning to get anxious about the long absence of the weans when they appeared from the melee.

'I'll be glad when I get this perr safely hame...' declared James, thanking his friend and putting the treasured watch in his pocket. They had chosen toys to share; a large jigsaw puzzle and a package containing two bats and a ball.

'We'll keep them at your house Granda,' explained Sonny.

James had a mind picture of the two locked in battle over the toys. However he smiled cheerily and led them away from the Barras. Now for the People's Palace. They had been to the Museum several times, but never tired of gazing at all the things from a bygone era. Some not so old, like Billy Connolly's banana boots, they giggled over. They wondered at the wee old kitchen from long ago. Granda explained that it was similar to his grandmother's tenement flat, with the set-in bed and the shiny black range with the coal fire on which she had cooked meals for her large family.

Back down the stairs, Sonny voiced regret that all these interesting models of engines and ships were behind glass.

James breathed a sigh of relief at the thought of it safely out of the reach of Mister Footerie Fingers.

They went to the snack bar, under the glass roof, sharing the space with a beautiful tropical garden. Norma was already there holding the tray.

'I'm starving,' she announced. It was a lovely snack, milkshakes for them and coffee for Granda, sandwiches and a slice of their favourite fruitcake.

Later they walked through the Green and down to the river and sat, basking in the sunshine. The boy had kept some bread for the ducks, but the ever-hungry pigeons fluttered around them. One sat on Norma's shoulder. She was delighted. Granda was not! He shooed the bird away. 'Aw, ye frightened the wee soul.'

'Your mother won't be too pleased if you get bird shit on your good jacket!'

The pigeon circled aloft, plop! Something landed on granda's bunnet. The two wee terrors collapsed giggling on the seat.

'Oh, Granda, a doo's dunnit on yir bunnet!'

James removed his soiled headgear and attempted to wipe the offending mess with some tissues. He smiled wryly as he dropped the tissues in the bin.

'Come on you two before we get dive-bombed again. I've just remembered the bunnet for Sonny.'

'I don't need one,' said Sonny.

'Ye do, cause ye don't want to wear the one wi' the toorie that Gran knitted you for nursery school,' teased Norma.

'Of course not,' said Granda, 'he is at the big school now, mind you. Have to walk up our windy hill in winter.'

The boy loved the corduroy hat in the window, brown it was, with a skip and ear flaps. It sat on top of his baw heid!

Norma giggled and Granda snatched it off. 'It's too wee!'

Sonny glowered and tried to retrieve the prized helmet.

'Do you have this in a larger size?'

'Sorry sir, it's the only one.' The assistant was very helpful and displayed an assortment of headgear.

The wee lad was set on the brown corduroy, nothing else

would do. They finally left the shop hatless.

'Your mammy can take you for a bunnet next Saturday.'

James was beginning to feel the strain!

Back home, he sat down in his chair and closed his eyes, too tired to open his newspaper, oblivious to the noise and laughter from the back green, as his daughters supervised the tennis game.

A rope between two clothes poles as a net, and the weans whacked the ball back and forth.

In the kitchen, Grandma stirred the tea and chatted about her shopping expedition. She came into the living room with James's Celtic mug, strong sweet tea the way he liked it.

'How was your afternoon?

A rumbling blissful snore was the answer. She smiled as the noise in the back green escalated,

'Och, aye,' she said fondly, 'they are a bit of a handful.'

The Ferrymaster

Kenny McCallum

IT'S ALL HALLOW'S EVE ON THE
YOKER FERRY
SAILING AT THE WITCHING HOUR
OCTOBER 31st
ALL CHILDREN WELCOME
BRING A TREAT FOR THE FERRYMASTER

Children of all ages from Hillhead to Clydebank, from Partick to Dalmuir, were brought by mums, dads, aunts and uncles to Wolbirn's Wharf.

The ferry looked spectacular: lanterns, spooky faces glowing, each one with a different expression, candles set inside the gouged bellies of pumpkins; eerie flickering disturbed only by an occasional breeze; masks hung from overhead ropes, waiting for their guests, distributed evenly around the boat. Between the bright moon and the glowing lanterns, some of the masks gave the disturbing look of eyes scanning from side to side.

One by one the children, dressed up for the occasion – with more witches and ghouls covered in white sheets than could be counted – dropped apples, oranges, handfuls of monkey nuts, and little iced sponge cakes (icing piped to show scary faces with red, upturned lips) into the large basket, their treats for the Ferrymaster.

Bowing to each boy and girl as they eagerly placed their fare inside the wicker container, the black-hooded figure waved them aboard. No one took any notice of the pointing skeletal finger. A few of the livelier children tried to peer inside the black hood, but came away only with a contented smile, as if privy to an age-old secret.

The older relatives were huddled in groups, chatting, exchanging gossip, giving only an occasional glance at their offspring or charges for the evening. All aboard, the ramp slowly lifted. The old rusted bell swung, the clanger counting out thirteen ominous, echoing strokes. There was no way back...

Suddenly, a chill enveloped the ferry. A thick mist appeared, darkening the sky, pushing its way through the crowded deck, thickening, filling out every space it could find, as the chug, chugging of the engine pulled the craft away from land.

The kids were laughing... shouting... playing. The adults were growing concerned, unable to see anything around them. Soon, nothing would concern them again...

The engine stopped. The grind of the huge chain, which kept the ferry in line for the crossing, made no more cranking noises.

Girls and boys stood rigid, looking around in silence, sensing something amiss. The ferry drifted, as if in wide open sea. Like a huge blanket, the fog began to lift, unveiling the eerie outline of shapes it had encompassed. It hung in the air above like giant paper cut-outs of figures strung across the dark night sky.

No land could be seen ahead. It was as if the ferry had turned, parted from its link with Renfrew and was floating down the Clyde.

At first the children stood with worried expressions. No adults could be seen. They were alone... A snigger was heard, then another. Before long a full bodied laugh rippled through the air. Boys and girls joined in with the hysterical, infectious laughter as it surged along like a fast moving tide.

Kids were pointing, but not at the same place. Each was looking at his or her own particular pumpkin.

Staring out from each of the glowing heads, were the faces of mums, dads, aunts and uncles.

*

Each year, on Hallowe'en as the clock strikes midnight, laughter can be heard drifting across the Clyde. Some say you can see the flickering of the lanterns, as the ferry glides along, under the Erskine Bridge.

Why not come down to Wolbirn's Wharf at Hallowe'en? But remember to bring a treat for the Ferrymaster!

I'll be waiting...

Alice
Saket Priyadarshi

The week began with warnings – trivial little mishaps that were, in fact, omens in disguise. But Alice was too focused on Friday, on surviving to the week's end, to notice the signals that the future sent. She didn't think to prepare herself. Monday, as usual, wasn't nearly as bad as she had dreaded; although driving home from work, she was almost trampled by one of those modern, silvery jeeps. Her front right indicator had stopped blinking. Just another near thing, she sighed, dismissing the incident; and going to the garage – another task to be crammed into the future. She awoke on Tuesday breathing frosty fumes and panicked. The room was a morgue. The air was icy, her sheets stone cold, the radiators – dead. The pilot light just wouldn't stay lit. Get a plumber and phone work. Nothing else for it. She calmed quickly. Took it in her stride. And it proved to be no more than a minor irritation. The plumber was there in thirty minutes, had it fixed within an hour and, best of all, hardly spoke a word. He kindly left her the bill. She could send the cheque by post. Didn't waste his breath with *know where to find you* and all that. A reasonable charge too. Not a disaster, just the usual spanner in the works a fortnight before payday. She coped with the hassle, felt calm running through her veins. In control.

Alice hummed a melody, an old, old melody, as she set off for the office so late that morning. She was grateful for the few extra hours at home in which she had tended, at last, to her plants whilst waiting for her boiler to be tickled back to life. She basked in the relative freedom of the roads. It was the lull between the rush hours. A boorish caller on the radio even made her smile. Could he be the reticent boiler man of her morning? Letting off steam? At the lights, she caught her transparent image giggling on the glass of a car next to hers. She saw the smile the reflection wore and felt it broaden on her own face. She examined herself – straightened her glasses, ignored the grey hairs. She was better. Getting better every day. Coping with trials and tribulations. Just like everyone else. But on Wednesday the letter arrived and with it, as if through the letterbox, the past, like a flood. And after that the days, the hours, the minutes slowed. Down. By Friday, facing work was an impossibility. The flat remained dark and still, the curtains closed. She lay under the duvet. Warm and safe. At least there was comfort in that. She lay under the duvet pulled right up to her chin, clutching David against her cheek, crying.

Crying against the jar. Tears against the jar. Salt on clay dissolves the clay. Burns a hole right through it. A hole right through to David. Her David, Young David, in a jar with a hole. Hold the lid. Hold the lid tight. Spill. Sneeze and he's everywhere. Like dust to dust in the dusty air. Crazy thoughts. Tears don't go through clay. And it's an urn not a jar. Crazy thoughts. Why would she sneeze? Crazy thoughts against the urn with her head against the urn. Earn the good days, Alice. Pay. Pay pain. The pain. Loss. Forever. Think back, Alice. Before forever. Smile. Force it. Think straight. Normal thoughts. Happy thoughts. Ignore the pillow beating. Heart-beating. Ignore that taste. It's tears, Alice. Tears. Salt that burns a hole. A hole right through to David.

It was dying without dying. Her flat buzzed with silence. The darkened rooms held still as if not even time moved through them. She lay curled and fixed, smothered in the comfort of her bed, clinging to an urn, every muscle seized by a fear of moving. She was drowning without drowning and this time it was strong. Nothing to live for. Over. Crazy thoughts gurgling in her head. Solutions. Thin rope cutting into her neck as she hung from the clothesline. Blackness. She was sweating. It was panic and terror. Think straight, but ill feelings came with thoughts of their own, solutions whispered by a mad voice. You're buried alive. Can't go on like this. The window – just close your eyes. Jump! Dread, palpitations and fear, all night. It was loneliness with a voice that talked of only one thing – she was drowning without drowning and why did she fight it?

But Alice had been through this before, many times. Often enough to have discovered the secret to why it was her that was still alive. Despair, she had learnt, came like a compulsion. She had little choice in how or when. Something as minor as an innocent comment from a stranger, or witnessing a malice in the street, or even a letter from the Fiscal stating the obvious, could trigger it. And it came like a flood and swept her away. Crazy thoughts swimming inside her and she drowning in them. Even if she had read the omens and prepared herself, she had no control over its beginning. Nor could she resist despair as its current inevitably grew stronger. But the thing was, and this was the secret, it was the same with the will to live. It, too, was no more than an inexplicable urge. And the very things that pushed her to the edge of the end – events and words, people and ideas – the workings of life, came like little miracles, to rescue her when she was drowning, to pull her aboard the turning world, to move her on from this time to the next, and to restore her to her better self.

On Saturday morning, the phone rang. Three and half rings and then her sister's voice crackled through the answering machine. Electricity now buzzed through the flat. Margaret saying:

'Alice, you must be getting ready. I'm really sorry but I'm running a tad late so... Give me half an hour and I'll be there. Bye.'

That's all it took: a familiar voice, a charge in the air. Alice put away the urn and rose. She was out the shower and dressed in minutes. She opened her bedroom curtains and gave herself half a minute to bathe in the cold, grey light of autumn. As the kettle boiled and the bread toasted, she let the day into every room. After a rushed breakfast, her tablet and then she was ready, waiting on the steps outside when Margaret veered into view. Alice took a deep sigh and waved. She couldn't have done this last month. Such a quick recovery and the madness of the last few days lay hidden and silent behind her.

Mother was fine. She recognised both of them that day. She even commented on the carnations Alice bought on the way to the Home. (Although only to say how faded and dull they looked.) Afterwards, they sighed in sibling exasperation as they walked to *The Greeting* – the same café that mother had treated them to every Saturday afternoon for years. They placed their regular order: toasties and salads, diamond cakes and lattes (where scones and tea used to be). And as they waited, the talking:

'So Alice, how are you?'

Alice reached into her handbag and gave the letter to Margaret. Surprising how easy it was. For once, she hadn't tried to hide her panic by being the one to ask the first and second and third questions. For once, she hadn't looked away when asked how *she* was. Margaret read the letter from the Fiscal:

Dear Mrs Dean,

Further to our previous correspondence and in particular to your last letter of ——, I can now inform you that all outstanding tests with regard to determining the cause of death of your son David Alexander Dean have been completed. Their findings have been forwarded to me today and as it is my duty to keep you up to date, I am writing to you immediately. The most recent reports confirm the findings of the first. Namely: that there is no reason to doubt the cause of death as stated on Mr David Alexander Dean's Death Certificate as issued on ——. Furthermore, I have discussed the findings with the pathologist responsible and he informs me that he is quite unequivocal as to the fact that your son David did indeed die of an accidental overdose of heroin self-administered intravenously on the night of ——.

The pathologist-in-question's details and his full written report have been forwarded to your legal representative ————. However, I wished to communicate with you directly in order to convey the seriousness with which your concerns were regarded and the thoroughness of subsequent investigations. I hope you will agree that the matter is now closed.

Finally, I have asked your legal representative to contact us with regard to the disposal of the pathological specimens, which are currently in our safe keeping.

Yours Sincerely,

Margaret folded the letter and took Alice's hand.

Alice agreed to an afternoon at Margaret's. And what's more, when there she allowed herself to be shoved up the stairs by Allyson. Her teenage niece wanted advice on make up and trusted an aunt who never used any more than a mother who wore too much. Margaret's husband fixed Alice a martini so strong that she would have usually nursed it all night, but she emptied her glass in half an hour and found herself asking for – '*A repeat prescription*!' She stayed for dinner and had already made up her mind that this time she would accept the inevitable offer of the guest room and one of her sister's nighties when it came. Best of all was her self control when she saw Peter. He was only a year older than David and carried that same kind manner. There he stood in a yellow satin top and jeans, just back from the pub. So many young men would have run a mile from their derailed aunt who clung on to them in memory of their own lost son, but not Peter. He rushed over to Auntie Alice, gave her a big wet one on the cheeks, and nestled down beside her on the sofa. He even surrendered his hand. Tonight, she returned it to his lap after no more than a reasonable few minutes.

That night, in the guest room of her sister's house wearing borrowed pyjamas and having skipped brushing her teeth, Alice closed her eyes and within seconds sank into sleep. Soon, she was driving. A long and unfamiliar road stretched out ahead. She was traversing the countryside. Green pastures and distant hills, but somewhere she had no memory of having visited. The sky was patchy-blue and grey. Why she was driving and where to was a mystery. A riddle she had just begun to contemplate when a bus, travelling in the same direction, came alongside her car. She turned away from the road to look at the bus. It was half full and every passenger had come to the window to look back at Alice. And she knew each and every one of them. The window seats were taken by women and behind them were the men, either standing in the bus' aisle or kneeling on the seats. Granny and Grandpa Philpott then Granny Wright, as pale as in her coffin. Mother and father were there, together. She waving and him nodding knowingly as if he'd just caught little Alice out again. And David stood behind them, laughing. He tapped his grandpa's shoulder and pointed to her. They chuckled as if sharing some private joke. He looked happier than she could remember ever seeing him. Auntie Finny and Uncle Jack just smiled. May, her old Cockney neighbour from their days down South, showed her nicotine brown teeth. Even Doris and Tim, her ex-husband's parents, were aboard. Her – timid and ill at ease, and him – erect and to attention. They'll never change, thought Alice, not even there. And so many other faces: Bob, her window cleaner in Ayr, and Sue, her colleague who died of cancer. Mr Carruthers, the old school head who had disappeared one weekend – the first death she could remember; and little Sally – her friend from the close who couldn't even say leukaemia. A motley crew if ever there was one. But they seemed to be enjoying their excursion and what's more they seemed so pleased to have come across Alice. They could not take their eyes off her and nor she from them. They wore such benevolent, such joyful expressions. Alice let the car drive itself and feasted on the faces she had loved. It was only a dream, after all.

A Visit to Port Carlisle and Silloth July 2000

Jim Trevorrow

Indolent sheep lay amongst the buttercups and lush grass, like old women in repose, chewing the cud beneath the grey trunked beech trees, and in the shelter of the thorn hedges. So overgrown were the latter, that it was hard to tell which was hedge and what was undergrowth, verdant in the July heat. Meadowsweet, with its candyfloss cream flowers and fragrant pervading perfume, vied with clumps of ferns and blue vetch, erupting in huge bunches of colour hanging from amongst the hawthorn. Tall pink spikes of foxgloves pointing to the sky fought for ascendancy with the white marguerite. Dandelion, coltsfoot, purple thistles, ragwort, higher above the verge than is usual, mingled with the old English briar rose, intertwined with sweet scented honeysuckle. Then there were clusters of fiery willow herb and those high stalks of wild parsleys and hogweeds, with tall stems and white plate-like flowers; which as children we carelessly lumped together under the term Dog's Flourish. Lastly, an infinite array of grasses, uncut, tall and seeding, made it hard to identify the hawthorn that provided the frame and home for them all.

To the North lies the sea, so we believed, though to the eye it appeared as though we could walk across to Scotland, the two lands loomed so close together, were it not for a tiny strip of sand and water – the salty Solway itself. Gulls flocked together like vultures, gathering above the quicksands and tidal races, a living warning to the deceitful eye. Cattle wandered aimlessly between them and the road, cropping and grazing the grass on the marshes, or lay somnolent under a threatening sky. Clouds, dirty curdled grey, and white as milk, tumbled down over the ceiling, shadowing the light. Sprinkled along the coast the notices read:

WARNING. BATHING IS DANGEROUS OWING TO FAST RUNNING CURRENTS AND TREACHEROUS SANDS.

What use then, in such an emergency, would be those red painted life belt rings, hanging idly from the boards?

Farther on along the coast, the tide was reaching out to sea. In its ebb and retreat, it left crescent necklaces of sand around the bays. Little outcrops of red sandstone rock lent their distinctive colour to the shore, so seductive to the unwary, with its promise of redgold space.

Author Biographies

Lois Brooks studied languages and taught English abroad in the eighties and worked as a BBC subtitler in Glasgow in the nineties. She now hopes to concentrate on writing. She is a member of the Dept of Continuing Education evening class in creative writing at Strathclyde University.

Nick Brooks is thirty-three, lives in Glasgow and was recently awarded an SAC bursary to buy time to write. His Spanish is quite rusty, and his Portuguese is rotten. He is currently writing a novel. He has recently completed his MLitt in creative writing at the Edwin Morgan Centre, Glasgow University.

Kathy Daly lives in Paisley. She attends a creative writing class at Strathclyde University. This is her first story to be published. She is not working on the great Scottish novel, just yet. She is married with a son.

Jen Hadfield lives in Glasgow, calling herself a writer but mainly sells cheese. She has recently completed her MLitt in creative writing at Glasgow University.

Ingrid Lees grew up in East Berlin, escaped to West Germany and soon moved to London where she trained as a nurse and midwife. She has worked in Britain, Germany and East Africa. She is married with four daughters and works in Glasgow as a German language tutor at Glasgow University. She writes prose and poetry and gives creative writing workshops. She was a member of Pollokshields Writers and is a facilitator at Survivors' Poetry.

Kenny McCallum was born in Glasgow in 1963 and is a member of Drumchapel Writers' Group. His first short story, *Girls On Top*, was published in *Nomad 7* alongside Edwin Morgan. He is currently working on a Glasgow thriller for children.

Rena McEwan is a member of the Botanic Gardens Writers' Group and contributed to their publication *Microwaves* earlier this year. She was born and grew up in Glasgow, then lived in Perth for 28 years before returning to Glasgow in 1997. She has four grown up children.

Roberta McLellan was born in Glasgow. She started writing three years ago when she became a member of the Kinning Park writers. This is her first published story.

Tony McLean was born in Glasgow in 1966, and has a story published in *New Writing Scotland 19.*

Martin MacIntyre attended Pollokshields Writing Group during 1999/2000, but has now returned with his wife and daughter to live in Edinburgh. He writes short prose, poetry and tells stories in English and Gaelic. He has had a number of items published and is under commission to complete a bilingual collection of short stories and poems.

Anne Maley is a senior citizen of Glasgow. She was born in 1921. With her husband James, she has raised a fine family of nine. Anne is a member of the Maryhill creative writing class. She has had short stories published and is in the process of writing a novel.

Kenny Manley lives in Dalmuir and took an interest in writing while working for Glasgow libraries, and through Pollok library's writing group. This is his first published story.

Margaret Merry Robertson Mansell was born in 1960. She lives in Glasgow and has four sons. She graduated in July 2000 with a BSc (Hons) in Interior Design. Her interest in writing short stories and poems began this year, after joining Pollok Writers' Group.

Laura Marney has had stories published in *Cutting Teeth, Northwords, Spoke, Cencrastus, Nomad* and *Nerve*. Recently finished the MLitt course at Glasgow and Strathclyde in creative writing, currently finishing her first novel.

David Pettigrew was born in Kilmarnock in 1971. He wrote *Pipe Dreams* while attending the creative writing class at Strathclyde University. It is his first published story.

Saket Priyadarshi was born in India and is now a Southsider. Married and gainfully employed by the government, he enjoyed a short stint as a travel writer (*Sunday Herald, Scotsman*) but prefers fiction. He is awaiting broadcast of a short story on BBC Radio 4. He attended the Open Studies Evening Class in creative writing at Strathclyde University.

Sheila Puri was part of Pollokshields Writing Group. She has had stories published in *Chapman, New Writing Scotland,* and broadcast on BBC Radio Scotland. She works in Social Work, has two children and tries to grow French beans in-between writing stories.

E K Reeder was born in Chicago and has lived in Scotland for eight years. She was shortlisted for the Macallan/*Scotland on Sunday* prize in 1998, has been published in other anthologies and journals, and has just completed her first novel.

Jas Sherry is currently putting together collections of both short stories and poems, as well as working on various text and music projects. He is a member of Otherwise, a group of writers, artists and musicians and was formerly a member of Southside writers. He is on the MLitt course in creative writing at Glasgow and Strathclyde Universities.

Jim Trevorrow is a member of Easterhouse All Writers. He was born in Glasgow in 1936. He spent ten years in commerce and then studied Divinity. He was a youth worker in London. His ministries were in Edinburgh, Corby (Northants), Islay and Glasgow. He is married with three children, five grandchildren and two cats.

If you live in Glasgow, are a writer, or would like information on joining a writers' group, contact:

The Literature Development Officer
Mitchell Library
North Street
Glasgow
G3 7DN

About 11:9

Our aims

Supported by the Scottish Arts Council National Lottery Fund and partnership funding, 11:9 publish the work of writers both unknown and established, living and working in Scotland or from a Scottish background.

11:9's brief is to publish contemporary literary novels, and is actively searching for new talent. The work does not have to be set in Scotland. If you wish to submit work send an introductory letter, a brief synopsis of your novel, a biographical note about yourself and two typed sample chapters to: Editorial Administrator, 11:9, Neil Wilson Publishing Ltd, Suite 303a, The Pentagon Centre, 36 Washington Street, Glasgow, G3 8AZ. Details are also available from our website at **www.11-9.co.uk.**

If you would like to be added to a mailing list about future publications, either register on our website or send your name and address to 11:9, Neil Wilson Publishing Ltd, Suite 303a, The Pentagon Centre, 36 Washington Street, Glasgow, G3 8AZ

Books can be bought from our website, **www.11-9.co.uk**, any good book shop, or direct from our distributor: 0131 229 6800.